The Sleeper Awakens

June Whatley

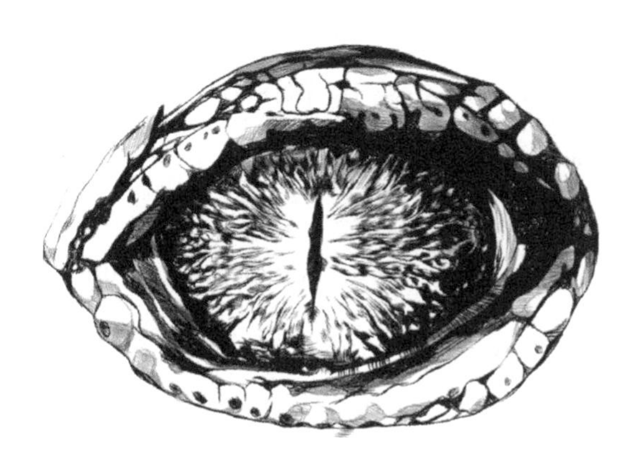

Published by Jurnee Books, an imprint of Winged Publications

ISBN: 978-1-952661-57-0

Dedication

This book is dedicated to the four greatest Grands in the world.

Josiah, Emily, Zion Grace, and Miriam.

Table of Contents

Acknowledgments

I want to thank my Beta Readers for their help and encouragement.

Audrey A. from Knoxville, TN was my first Beta Reader. She started with me when she was twelve-years-old. She had wonderful insights and stuck with me through all of my drafts. Thanks Audrey, you were (and are) a blessing.

Also, many thanks to Ana Ruth G., Tiffany G., Rebekah G., and Michaela G. from Fairmount, IN, for their wonderful suggestions and encouragement. Without sweet people like you, I couldn't have done this. You are all blessings.

Special thanks to Jedidiah J. from Stafford, VA. I really appreciate the fact that you liked the book cover and wanted to read the book. Blessings!

Many thanks to John Andrew B. of Dunlap, TN for his help and encouragement by being a Beta Reader.

Thank you to my mentors and friends at Serious Writer Club. I have learned a great deal from you. I know I have much more to learn, but you kept me going. Blessings!

Thank you, Lord for your salvation, love and forgiveness. I am nothing without you.

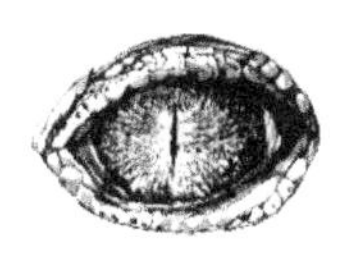

Chapter 1

Drone or Dove?

Ashton slapped his brother on the back, *swakkkk.* "That's what y'get for trying to leave me home again. And 'tag, you're it,' Slime-ball."

Only a microscopic movement, a tiny flinch, betrayed Mican's pain, then nothing; he didn't chase him, or yell, or anything.

Beside Mican, Shayla stood stone-still, like a statue.

"Hey, Snot-wads, whatever you're staring at can't be that great." The next second proved him wrong, Ashton's eyes locked onto a bizarre sight.

He now beheld the strange distraction that captivated his brother and sister. “Whoa! That’s mega-weird!”

Shayla’s eyes flashed toward her brother as she jerked her finger to her lips. “Shhhhh, Ashy. You might scare it.”

A few feet ahead of them, in the midst of the trees, a pure white dove hovered above the path. The bird’s satiny feathers reflected the sun’s rays; the golden-brown beak pointed directly at them like the needle of a compass.

Its dark, beady eyes remained fixed on Mican who stood spellbound, not a wiggle, not even a breath could be detected until he spoke. “That bird doesn’t seem to be afraid at all, Shay. I have the strangest feeling it wants me to follow it.”

Shayla gasped. “What? No! Mican, you can’t. Please. I think Ashy’s right. That bird’s weird.”

Ashton darted to cover the short distance between himself and his siblings. He craned his neck toward the bird. “I’m not even sure that thing’s real, dude. Look how it’s just hangin’ there. It’s not even flappin' its wings. Do y'think it could be a drone? Man, I wish I'd brought my binoculars."

Mican glanced at his brother, his eyebrows scrunched. "What binoculars?"

Ashton's cheeks dimpled into a wide smile, but he didn't answer, he continued to study the bird. "I just gotta know what that thing is."

Step-by-step, he edged forward. Halfway, he turned his head to the side. After a moment, he glanced back. "So far, I can't hear a motor. I'm gonna try to see if it has a camera in its eye." Again, he inched his way toward the bird. When close enough, he extended his index finger.

The stern voice of a man snapped at him. "Move. Your. Finger. I assure you I am real. I am not a drone. And I do not have a camera in my eye."

Ashton staggered back two steps. "Who said that?"

The dove flitted in front of him. "I did."

"No way!" Ashton's head wobbled side-to-side. "Birds can't talk."

The dove fluttered in so close, Ashton's eyes

crossed. "It would seem, Ashton, where I am concerned, you are mistaken."

"How'd y'know my name?" Ashton leaned back to clear his eyesight. "That's just plain ol' T-rex-amous scary."

In a calm voice, the dove lifted his chin and answered. "The King told me who you are. I've been sent to find the three of you and bring you to him."

Ashton's hands flared at his sides. "What king?"

But Mican interrupted. "So, you … are looking … for us?"

The bird faced Mican's direction. "Well certainly. Who else would I be looking for in the woods behind your house?" His feathers ruffled slightly as he fluttered in closer. "I told you, I have been dispatched by the King to usher you to him. Are you coming or not?"

When Mican glanced from his brother to his sister, he noticed how stiff their bodies appeared. He issued a challenge. "Why are you two so worried? We have a talking bird here. Aren't you curious? Or are you too scared to follow him to see where he goes?"

"We're not scared, we're just …." Ashton stammered for a moment.

Shayla finished for him. "We're surprised, that's all."

Ashton peered at her and mumbled from the corner of his mouth. "I was thinkin' more like we're weirded-out."

The dove turned to fly into the woods. "Are you coming or not?"

Mican swept his hand through the air. "Come on, you two, let's see where he takes us. Don't you want to meet this King-guy?" He trotted to catch-up with the dove and yelled back, "Last one in is a rotten raptor egg."

He zipped away from his sister, who kicked into high gear.

Ashton dashed to catch up. "Don't go without me."

With his sister now close behind him, Mican tossed out a little taunt. "His FOMO is kicking in."

A shout erupted from behind them. “I don’t have FOMO. You take that back, dog-face!”

Mican chuckled.

Shayla corrected him. “Don’t be mean, Mican. You don’t know what it’s like to be afraid of missing out. You’re popular at school, Ashy’s not.”

“You’re right, Shay-belle. I’m sorry.”

“Don’t tell me, bubba. Tell Ashy,” said Shayla.

For the next several minutes, they followed the dove through the forest. Tall trees allowed sunlight to seep down through the bare branches, while the slight shade protected them from too much sun. The touch of a gentle breeze pushed past them.

Without warning, Mican stopped. Shayla bumped into him, which forced Ashton to stop short. “Hey! Watch it, Booger-brain!”

Mican shouted to the dove. “Hey bird, stop a minute. How much farther are you taking us?”

The dove turned and flew toward them.

A sweet puff of air washed over their faces as the bird flitted in close.

Staring Mican squarely in one eye, the bird

answered. "If you don't follow me, you will never know what could have been."

Shayla grabbed her brother's arm. "That bird's scaring me. Maybe we should go home."

Mican's eyes remained locked on the bird hovering in front of him. "What do you mean, if we don't follow you, we will 'never know what could have been'?"

"I can only tell you what the King has instructed me to say."

Through gritted teeth, Ashton asked, "What King? Who *are* you?"

The dove redirected his attention. "Ashton, you have an invitation from the King. I have been sent to show you the way to the castle. You must follow me to learn more. Follow or don't follow. You must choose."

Shayla gasped and staggered, toppling into Ashton.

"I said, watch it, Airhead," then he shoved her.

Mican turned to face her and placed his hands on her shoulders. "Calm down, Shay. Let's at least see where he takes us. I would like to meet a real King. Wouldn't you?"

She swished her hair from side-to-side. "I don't know, bubba. I'm scared."

Ashton chimed in. "I don't know either. It's too, y'know, too freaky."

Shayla stared into Mican's eyes. "But I will follow you, bubba, if you think we should follow the bird."

The dove addressed her. "No, Shayla. Each of you must make your own decision."

Mican straightened to face his brother. "You heard him, Ash. We each have to make our own decision. I would like to see where the bird takes us, but what do you think?"

Pinching his chin, he puckered his lips and nodded. "I'll give it a try. If he starts anything, I think I can beat up a bird." He tossed his head back and laughed.

The dove lifted his feathered head and raised one eye. "That certainly will not be necessary, young man." The bird looked toward Mican, but did a quick second glance at Ashton.

Mican stared into the face of his cherished, little sister. "What's your vote, Shay-belle? Would you like to follow him or not?"

Staring at the ground, she fidgeted. "I'm afraid he's going to try to kidnap us, or to get us into some kind of trouble."

Fluttering in close to her, the dove softened his voice. "I promise, child, I am not trying to kidnap you, and I definitely will not get you into trouble … *if* you follow me."

She tilted her head to make eye contact with her brother. "I guess it's okay then, since he promised."

Mican addressed their feathery guide. "We will follow you," but added, "as long as we feel safe."

The dove shook his head, fluffed his wings, and replied with great excitement. "Fair enough. This way, please."

A crisp breeze stirred the branches of the trees. The smell of newly emerging greenness filled the air. Mican followed a few feet behind the dove. Shayla trailed after him, with Ashton close on her heels.

Questions plagued Ashton's mind. How far will this bird take 'em? Is Shayla right—could they be in danger? What kind of trouble could be waiting for them ahead?

He swatted the air in front of his face. Nonsense, that's craziness. Nothing could go wrong. They knew every inch of these woods. They've played here many times. Deep in thought, Ashton followed the others into a clearing.

The dove stopped and hovered in front of a large, stone wall. Gray stones peeked from beneath dried vines and branches. It looked as if it had once been the boundary of an ancient fortress, but now abandoned.

Ashton's mouth sagged open. He stared for a second, then said, "Look at those big, ol' rocks. They are stacked without even a crack between 'em." He compared it to the height of his brother. "And that wall is almost three feet higher than your head, bruh. It must be at least eight feet high."

Mican gestured toward the barrier, but asked the

dove, "Is this for real? That wall, I mean? And the trees around us are full of leaves, but behind us, spring has barely started. What is this? Where are we?"

Ashton nodded in agreement, pointed at the bird and shouted. "You heard him, answer my brother. Where are we? We know every inch of these woods," he flung his hand toward the wall, "but we've never seen *that* before."

Unruffled, the dove answered. "You have never followed me before." Using his wing to point at a place heavily covered with twisted vines and dead branches, the dove's chipper voice delivered a simple request. "Pull, please."

Ashton carefully gripped a piece of vine, needled with thorns. He glanced over his shoulder at the dove, but the bird repeated the instruction. "Pull, please."

At first, Ashton tugged gently, but nothing happened. Using two hands, he pulled again. Still nothing moved.

Mican rubbed his chin. "Put your foot against

the wall for more power, dude."

His brother placed one foot against the wall, leaned back, and strained. "You mean…like…this?" His face scrunched, while he struggled. When a piece of dry vine broke free, he tumbled backward and sprawled onto the ground. Ashton groaned.

Shayla and Mican laughed at their brother laying flattened in front of them.

"Bubba," Shayla laughed. "It looks like you are going to make a snow angel in the dirt."

He narrowed his eyes. "A little help here, Shay."

She extended her arm. "Give me your hand, bubba."

Mican walked over to help his brother up, then joined in the task of clearing away the dead limbs.

"Wow, cold stones, sharp thorns, and hard dry stems. Whatta job!" said Ashton.

They pulled, tugged, and got stuck by thorns as they attacked the twisted, woody branches.

After working hard for several minutes, Shayla

stopped. “All of this work is making me hot.” She pulled off her sweater and tied it around her waist.

Ashton copied his brother, who used his shirtsleeves to wipe beads of sweat from his forehead and upper lip, then rolled them up.

Not long after they returned to work, Shayla shrieked. “Ouch!” She jumped back and squeezed her hand where a large thorn stuck from her palm.

Ashton lifted one eyebrow and grinned. “Suck it up, Buttercup.”

Shayla wrinkled her lips. “Why are we doing this? And how much longer do we have to pull these stupid vines?”

The dove replied in his usual steady manner. “Until you can see.”

Ashton glanced at the bird and gave a mighty yank to the vine he held. “See what?”

The dove cooed and pointed. “That.”

Ashton stared at the spot where he had been working. “Hey guys, look at this. I can see somethin’ under here. It’s made outta wood and looks really old.”

Mican stepped over to his brother. “Wow.” He rubbed the bare spot of wood. “Let’s get back to work, so we can see what this is.”

They worked hard at the task of freeing the hidden treasure from its prison. With each snap and crackle of dried vines, more wood became visible. Beam-by-beam, an ancient barrier came into view.

When the final vine broke free in Ashton’s hands, he stepped back. “Guys, this is awesome. I’ve never seen such a beautiful gate in all my life.”

He touched the wood, examining it with an artist’s eye. “Look at these thick, heavy, beams. They’re so brown, they look like they’ve been stained. Y’know, like dad did to that ol’ desk in our room. And I guess, over time, the weather has worn ‘em smooth ‘cause I can’t feel a rough spot on ‘em anywhere.”

Mican leaned in to touch some metal on the gate. “Look at these hinges, they look like the metal roots of two trees. See how they reach up and down the side, but they don’t quite touch in the middle.”

Ashton stepped back for a better view. “And

look at that latch over there. It has so much detail carved into it. It looks like it's made of the same brassy material as the hinges." He almost whispered. "These must've been made by a master craftsman who works with metal."

Shayla ran her hand over a sign in the center of the gate. "Boys, look at the message carved into this board. The words are written in a strange, foreign-looking language."

Ashton patted a beam of the gate. The wood felt solid and warm. He inched his hand over the sign, sliding his fingers across the words, and traced the cuts of the letters. "These hollowed-out places are smooth, with no splintery edges. They feel like they've been cut by a laser." He turned to look at the dove. "What does this say?"

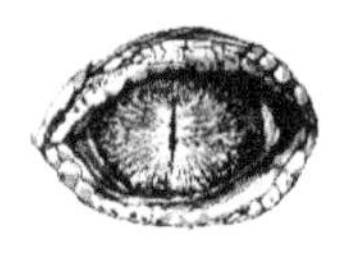

Chapter 2

The Dangerous Garden

Without answering Ashton's question, the dove fluttered to the side and hovered near the latch.

Mican placed his hands on his hips and fixed his eyes on the gate.

Shayla glanced at the bird, then to Mican. Her voice quivered. "Should we try to open it?"

Ashton stepped close to her, but stared at their older brother. "Since we've come this far, we should at least try it, don't y'think?"

Mican reached for the latch. "Here we go." His face twisted as he pushed and pulled, his knuckles turned white, and his voice strained. "This handle—doesn't look rusty, but—it—won't budge."

With his hand spread over the lower part of his face, Ashton tapped his foot. "Place one foot behind you and lean in toward the latch. See if it needs some tension taken off."

Mican placed his shoulder against the gate, his other elbow flared to the side as he worked at the handle, but nothing moved. He straightened and let out a heavy breath. "Still nothing."

Mican scratched his head and turned to the dove. "Does it need a key or something?"

"Not a physical key. If that's what you're asking."

Shayla grabbed Mican's sleeve and gave two short tugs. "Lift me up, so I can see over."

He winked at her and smiled. "Yes ma'am, Shay-belle." He bent his knees and laced his fingers together to make a stirrup. "Step into my hands."

She held onto his shoulders and with one foot firmly in his laced fingers, she pushed away from the ground. Mican straightened his knees and back to lift her, but as she reached for the top of the gate, it began to grow taller and taller. It continued to stretch out of her reach, no matter how high he lifted her.

Ashton shook his head. "A growing gate. No way, that *did not* just happen."

Carefully lowering Shayla, Mican bent his knees. With her hands on his shoulders, she jumped to the ground. He glanced at his brother. "Like it or not, Ash, it *did* happen."

Ashton pushed his brother aside. "Outta the way, Doofus. Let me try this stupid thing." He twisted, tugged, pushed, pulled, and grunted as he spoke. "This. Thing. Will not … open." Working with all of his might, he couldn't make the latch open either.

Mican scrunched his lips. "Well, isn't that a shocker, Ash?"

He stomped his foot and turned toward the dove. "Okay, bird. My hands are sore from pullin' vines and gettin' stuck by thorns; I'm in no mood for your riddles. How do we get in? Unless you brought us all the way here to show us a gate that won't open."

The dove answered, but remained calm. “You haven’t asked for it to be opened.”

Ashton wadded his hands into fists and plopped them on his hips. “You’ve gotta be kiddin’ me.”

Shayla faced the gate and held up her palms. “Gate, open.” But … no response. She stared at the dove.

“No, child. That is telling, not asking.”

She again turned to the gate, placed her fists at her waist and spat out the words. “Okay, gate, will you open?”

But still no movement of the latch.

Turning to the dove, she puckered her lips. “What did I do wrong that time?”

“Un-ball your fists please. Now ask politely.”

Again, she turned away from the dove to face the gate. She took her fists off of her hips and asked in a more pleasant voice. “Gate, will you open?” This time she added, “Pleeease.”

Still nothing happened. She whirled back around and stomped her foot. “So why didn’t it open that time?”

The dove moved in close to her. Cocking his feathered head, he tenderly replied. "Because, my dear, you didn't ask *me*."

She tipped her head back. "What? Are you serious?" Then she leveled her eyes at him. "Okay. Mr. Dove. Will *you* pleeease open the gate?"

He gently brushed the lock with the tip of his wing. The latch lifted and the gate drifted silently inward.

They glanced at each other before peering through the large opening.

Ashton stepped to the entryway, bent at the waist, leaning in he said, "It looks like a plain, ol' garden."

The bird led the way. "Believe me, young man, there is nothing plain' about this garden, though it is very 'old. Step inside, please."

Mican stood with his arm outstretched in front of Shayla. "Wait. You didn't answer Ash's question. What does the writing on the gate say?"

"You will be told, when it is time. One of you is not yet ready to hear. Now come this way, please."

Ashton and Mican both stared at Shayla.

All at once, her eyebrows arched up. “Well, don’t look at me. I’m ready.” And with a sudden move, she pushed his arm away and raced in.

“Shaaay-laaa, wait.”

But too late, she now stood inside the garden. Her mouth sank open and she spun around. “This is amazing!”

Mican rushed to her side.

“Wait for me!” Ashton lunged into the garden beside them.

The cheerful dove flew ahead. “Follow me, please.”

Mican tightened his lips and yelled at the bird. “Wait. Where are we and where are you taking us?”

“This is the King’s garden and I’m taking you to meet him, of course.”

While Mican focused on the dove, Ashton spotted an ugly creature creeping out of the bushes. Its nose ran and drool dripped from its mouth. A foul smell radiated from the beast.

Ashton tapped his brother’s shoulder. “Uhhh,

Mican."

Yanking away, he snapped, "What is it Ash?" But at that moment Mican *heard* the problem.

The grungy critter spoke with a harsh, grating voice. "Have you come to see my master?"

Shayla and Mican's heads jerked toward the strange voice, but when they saw the creature, they leaned away and froze.

Ashton managed to stammer. "We are here to meet the King. And we are, uhhhh, following the dove.

Without waiting, the dove swooped low to the ground between them and the creature and took charge. "Get out of our way, evil beast. I *know* who you are." He snapped an order at the animal. "In the name of the King, I command you to show your true self."

The hairs on their arms stood up when the ugly beast morphed into a large, grotesque reptile.

As the creature crawled toward them, his bumpy, gray scales rubbed together, creating a raspy noise. A pink lizard-like tongue flicked out.

Ugly yellow eyes locked onto them.

Shayla screamed and scrambled behind Mican. "Look! That nasty thing has wings."

At that moment, the beast leapt to take flight, heading straight for them.

With the speed of a bullet, the dove darted upward and spread his wings forming a shield between them and the wicked intruder. "Get out of our way, vile creature. Be gone. The King is waiting for us."

As if the bullet had hit its mark, the scaly reptile dropped to the ground with a thud. Grunting and hissing, the hideous animal slithered into the bushes and out of sight.

Just as quickly as his feathers were ruffled, the dove returned to his calm, peaceful nature. "Now children, we must be going. Come this way." He added, "You must be on your guard. Stay close to me."

Mican's body stiffened, his voice erupted. "You *promised* we would be safe."

The dove said, "And so, you are, dear boy. As

long as you stay with me, you will be quite safe. Come now." He fluttered a few feet ahead of them, above the smooth path.

Ashton tipped his head and gave his brother a questioning look. "Do you think we should keep followin' him?"

"Maybe it will be okay. We can always checkout if we think things aren't going right. Besides I have my cell phone, if we need it."

"Okay, does your phone have a full charge?"

He pulled it from his pocket. "Yep! Fully charged."

"Okay then. Better keep it handy."

He placed the phone back in his pants pocket.

While they walked along the path, Shayla glanced all around. "Bubbas, look at the pretty, flowers on both sides. They make the air smell wonderful. And do you hear the crickets, or whatever they are, chirping in the grass?"

"And y'know, this is weird," Ashton added, "the rustle of leaves make the trees sound like they're singing."

They followed along behind the dove, as the sound of flowing water drew closer. When they rounded the next bend, a gentle brook came into full view. It splashed and gurgled, straight ahead of them. Shayla rushed off the path, stepping into the rich, green grass that bordered the brook.

She twirled around and giggled. "Even the air around my ankles feels cooler. Boys, come look, the water is so clear I can see all the little pebbles in the bottom. They're such pretty colors and there are some fish swimming around too." Stretching up onto her tiptoes, she pointed downstream. "And over there, a frog is paddling along. He's so cute. Mican, I want to get a little closer. Is that okay?"

"Yeah, I guess so, but be careful."

Shayla stepped to the edge of the brook and stared into the water. "This looks so nice, I wish we had our swimsuits."

Several fish swam toward the bank and stared up at her. As she stared back, she pointed. "Look. That fish has the bluest eyes I've ever seen."

Five bubbles zigzagged to the surface. As they

reached the top of the water, each air pocket broke with a *bloop.* Shayla heard a word after each one. "What. Color. Are. Your. Eyes?"

She leaned over, placing her hands on her knees and laughed. "My eyes are brown."

The fish began to swim in a circle, then quickly reversed their course.

A large smile filled her face as she shouted to the fish. "Do you want to play?"

Bubbles broke the surface of the water with three *bloops* of, "Yes. Yes. Yes."

"Mican, I'm going to step off the bank onto this big rock. Here, hold onto me." She stuck her arm out to the side.

He grabbed her wrist and she used one foot to test the rock.

"It feels safe to stand on." When she placed both feet down, Mican released her arm.

From the bank, Mican and Ashton watched as some fish darted past Shayla's rock, then around another. Her eyes lit up; she glanced back at her brothers. "I think they want me to play Follow the

Leader. Can I?"

Mican lifted his shoulders. "I guess it'll be all right."

Shayla laughed and jumped onto another large stone.

It looked like so much fun, Ashton leapt onto his own large, flat rock.

Mican followed their lead.

The dove tried to intervene. "No, wait." But they weren't listening. He tried again to address them. "Children, no. Those fish are not what you think. Children stop!" But the gurgle of the creek and their laughter drowned out the dove's small voice.

Ashton tried to hop from one big stone to another, but when he landed, the rock wobbled and launched him into the water. *SPLASH!*

From where she stood, Shayla balled up her fist, leaned forward, and shouted at him. "You did that on purpose. You scared the fish."

He jumped to his feet to defend himself. "I did not." Water dripped from his clothes, sending ripples out with every droplet.

His brother's eyes narrowed and his voice blasted. "Yes, you did. You always try to get

attention."

Gripping his hands tight, Ashton stiffened his arm muscles and punched at the water. "No, I don't."

Mican shouted back. "Yes, you do. Why didn't you stay home?"

"You'd leave me out of everything if you could, like you tried t'do this morning." Ashton's face flashed hot. "You never want me around. And you always take *her* side. I wish she'd never been born. I wish you both had never been born. I want to be number one for a change, not the middle."

"You make that clear everyday by your actions, Ash, but why did you have to say it in front of Shayla?"

She stared at her feet. Her bottom lip puckered.

"Ash, you wonder why I don't want you around. Your actions and words are sometimes like poison. Now look at her. You hurt her feelings."

"I have feelin's too, y'know. I never get t'do what I want t'do, and you and the baby-girl are always hangin' around."

Mican crossed his arms and shouted. "If you don't want us *hanging around*, why do you always whine, 'Don't go without me.' Or 'Don't leave me.' You say you don't want us around, but you always include yourself in what we're doing."

Ashton leaned forward and shouted. "I just don't want t'be left out, that's all."

Mican leaned toward his brother and yelled at him. "Apologize to Shay."

"No, I won't. I wish I'd been an only child or at least the baby. I'm nothing and nobody loves me. You haven't even liked me since she was born. I remember you use to play with me."

"I try to watch out for Shay because you're always mean to her. The day Mom brought her home from the hospital, you tried to put her in the closet. You were always jealous, Ash."

"But you stopped loving me! Dad tried to make me feel better, but now he's gone."

Mican locked his hands into fists, then jabbed the air above his rock. “One of these days, Ash, you will be alone, then you’ll miss us.”

Ashton stared at him and gritted his teeth. “I can’t wait.” He snapped around and turned his back to his brother.

The dove flew between them and his small voice pleaded, “Boys, stop it right now. You are angry and you don’t mean what you are saying.”

At that moment a large, warty frog, from the opposite bank, leapt onto the rock next to Mican. In one quick bounce, Mican sprang to the far side of his rock.

With a gruff voice, the frog croaked, “Doesn’t matter if he fell in, we all need to get wet from time to time.”

The frog’s words sounded funny and Mican laughed. “Ash, turn around. Look. This frog makes a lot of sense. I guess he’s right. I’m sorry.”

Ashton glanced over and saw the frog, but waded out of the stream and stared down at his clothes. “Y’know what?” He lifted the front of his shirt away from his body. "I'm almost dry already."

His brother studied him head to toe and waved his hand. "You can't be. That's impossible."

Shayla stepped onto a rock near the bank, placed one hand on the grass, and reached with the other to feel Ashton's shirt. "It's true. He's almost dry."

Mican lifted his arms out to his sides. "If our clothes can dry that fast, …." He jumped into the water.

His brother grinned and followed. They began to laugh, splash, and play. Water went everywhere and the fish scattered.

The bird fluttered in a circle twittering. "Children, please, we must be going."

But it was no use. They weren't listening to the still, small voice of the dove.

Shayla pointed. "The fish are swimming away, let's follow them." She leapt from her rock into the water with her brothers and darted downstream, splashing wildly.

Mican and Ashton did the same.

From behind them came the dove's voice. "No, children .... Children, stop. We need to go upstream. You are being pulled away. We must get you to the King."

Again, they paid no attention to the dove.

They sloshed through the shallow water, chasing after the fish, but the further they went, the deeper the water got. The exercise of running in water became tiring and made Ashton hot, so he sat down in the now, knee-deep stream. He stretched his legs in front of him; the water rose up to his chest. A fish playfully jumped across him.

Shayla plopped down in the water, which came up to her chin. She placed the soles of her shoes against her brother's and kept her head tipped up to prevent the water from sloshing in her face. "Me too. Jump over me." She watched as one fish jumped over him and swam back to jump over her.

At that moment, Ashton noticed his brother who stood a few yards upstream. Mican's eyes squinted and he frowned. He glanced toward them, jerked his head the other way to look upstream, then turned their direction again and yelled.

Ashton cupped his hands to his mouth. “What? I can’t hear you.”

Mican hopped onto the bank. His feet began to dance up and down, but he stayed in one spot. He waved his arms and shouted again.

Ashton could tell he wasn’t joking. Finally, he heard his brother’s frantic voice. “Get out, Ash. Get out, Shay. They’re piranha.”

Ashton glanced around and realized he and Shayla had waded into a canyon. He immediately began to climb the bank, but slid back down the steep, muddy cliff. Shayla tried to scramble up, but also slid back again.

Mican ran along the stream and jumped into the water near his sister. He tried to push her up the bank, but the top edge crumbled away.

She wildly clawed at the dirt and screamed. “It’s breaking away, Mican. I can’t hold on!”

They couldn’t go back and if we went further downstream, the bank got even higher.” He grabbed Shayla by the arm and pushed her toward the opposite shore. Ashton quickly followed and they scrambled up the bank. They climbed out on the far side, just as the fish leapt out of the water and snapped at their heels.

Waving his hands over his head, Mican yelled, “Help dove. Help us.”

The bird flew to the middle of the brook, chirping as loudly as he could. “I tried to get you to follow me. I can’t cross over the stream. You will have to come to me.”

Shayla grabbed Mican’s arm with both hands. She stared up at him, tears filled her eyes. “I’m scared. The rocks in this part of the creek are too small to stand on, and the piranha are waiting for us if we fall in.”

Ashton squeezed his hands into fists. “Stupid bird, why can’t you cross over? You led us here.”

“I tried to get your attention, but you wouldn’t listen. I can’t cross over. That land is ruled by another.”

For a brief moment, Mican wrinkled his forehead, as his eyes stared into the distance. “It’s okay, guys. I have my cell phone. Ash, who do you think I should call, the police or mom?"

"Well duh, I don't think the fish have guns, so I don't think we need the cops. And what could Mom do? You should call the fire department, Nano-brain. Maybe they can bring a ladder to stretch across the creek. It's not that wide, it's just steep over there."

Shayla glanced up at him. "That's smart, Ashy, but you know Mican isn't a Nano-brain."

"Whatever, Booger-breath."

Mican pulled his phone from his pocket and pushed the buttons. "Oh no! My phone's not working." He felt his pocket. "My phone got wet when I jumped in to get Shay."

Ashton looked down. "I thought our clothes were supposed to dry fast." He planted his hands on his waist. "Okay, Dolt. What do we do now?"

His brother placed a thumb under his chin and tapped his cheek with his extended index finger, he cupped his hands and shouted to the dove. "I have a plan. It's easy. We will walk back upstream."

Mican pointed in the direction, then pulled his hand back to his mouth. “And we’ll look for a place to safely cross over. You can keep us in sight from your side until we come to the big rocks again. How does that sound?”

The dove’s eyes were knit close together. “Okay, but stay in sight at all times.”

They began their trip upstream, walking in silence. Not even crickets chirped on this side of the stream. There were no birds singing, no sound, except the babble of the water. An eerie silence engulfed them.

Mican’s eyes darted between the dove and the dangerous fish that trailed them at a distance.

Ashton scanned their surroundings. “Y’know, this place is creepy. It seems harder to walk over here too. I guess I’m just tired, but my body feels heavier than normal. And the grass is drier. Do y’think it gets less rain over here?”

“That doesn’t make any sense, Ash. Why would it rain less on one side of the creek than on the other?”

"I don't know, I was just thinking, that's all, but there's another thing. Where are the large rocks we used as steppingstones? Do you think someone took them out to keep us from crossing back over? I'm sure we should have reached the spot where I fell in by now."

After a short silence, Mican replied, "You know Ash, I have to agree with you there. I was thinking the same thing. But *surely* no one would take the stones out of the creek. That's impossible, right?"

Shayla interrupted. "Bubbas, wait up. Can we rest for a few minutes? My feet feel heavy."

Mican turned to Ashton. "Well, that part is not your imagination. Shay feels it too."

They waited for her to catch up. Mican cupped his hands to his mouth again and lifted his voice so the dove could hear him over the noise of the water. "We need to rest for a few minutes." He raised his fist; his thumb pointed over his shoulder. "We are going to move back away from the edge of the creek to be safe."

The dove fluttered to the center of the stream.

"Oh, I wish you wouldn't, but if you must, keep your eyes open and don't go too far. Stay where I can see you."

When Shayla caught up, they took a few steps away from the stream, but it didn't take long to discover their mistake.

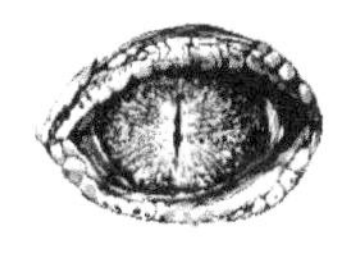

Chapter 3

Something Awaits

Shayla stretched out on the scratchy, dry grass. "I can't feel any breeze. Can you, bubba?"

Mican knelt beside her. "No, I can't either Shay. And the air feels dry and stuffy."

She glanced over at him. "I know what you mean, it is dry, but my clothes are still damp. I thought they would be dry by now."

He laid down with a grunt. "Oh man, I'm tired."

Shayla lifted her arms in front of her. "Look at me! My arms are streaked with mud from trying to climb that bank."

"It'll be okay, Shay-belle. Now rest."

Ashton stretched on his back with his ankles crossed, his fingers laced behind his head. "You should see your face, Shay-ding-a-ling. Why don't you go wash in the creek?"

Pushing onto her elbow, she shouted, "Stop it, Ash-booger. You *know* how scary those piranhas are. You ran too, remember."

"Hey, listen to your ten-year-old-sassy-self callin' me Ash-booger. I like it. I'm gonna keep that name." His belly arched as he laughed.

Shayla rolled the other way. "This place is so dark. And it smells funny. Nothing here seems alive." Her voice grew tense. "Boys, I'm getting a strange feeling that we're being watched."

Her brothers sat upright.

She craned her head toward the woods and without warning, some large insects came streaking toward them at a wild pace. She scrambled to her feet. "Run, Mican! Run, Ashy!"

They now saw why she yelled.

A swarm of large crab-shaped creatures flew out of the forest and jetted toward them. The insects' bulging eyes were set atop long stems that could turn in all directions. Long syphons, for mouths, enabled them to bite their victims without landing.

Mican, Ashton, and Shayla dashed through the forest, zigzagging their way through the dark, musty landscape. They ran, as fast as they could, without ramming into trees, as they batted and swatted their attackers, but still received vicious bites.

Mican swung wildly. “Some of these creatures are as big as my hand. I can’t kill them. They bounce off when I hit them, like the birdy in badminton.”

After several minutes, for no apparent reason, the swarm lifted and flew away. This gave them time to catch their breath.

Ashton held his arms out to examine them. “Man, these bites itch. Look at us. We have red spotty-bumps all over.”

Mican stood motionless, except to heave out a large breath through his mouth. When sufficiently recovered, he said, “Did you see the size of those things? I can’t imagine how big a mosquito hawk would have to be to eat one.”

Shayla panted. “What’s a mosquito hawk,

Mican?"

But Ashton offered an explanation. "It's a skeeter-eater, dummy. They're smaller than a dragonfly, but a lot bigger than a mosquito. I can't even guess how big one would have to be to eat one of those things. Maybe as big as a car door and meaner than a guard dog."

"Thanks for the help, Ash, but don't call Shay a dummy. Save your energy for something more useful. We need to keep watch in case those monsters come back and force us to have to run again. Keep your eyes open."

His brother covered one eye and in a gruff voice said, "Aye, aye, Capt'n Bligh."

They scratched their bites and rested, until Mican snapped out orders. "Come on, you two. We've rested long enough. We need to find our way back to the stream."

Ashton tipped his head back, scanning the treetops. "Have you guys noticed that no sunlight comes down through the trees over here? That makes it hard to see very far. Can anyone see the creek?"

Mican pondered for a moment, then pointed. "I think we should go this way. But keep your eyes open for the return of those Zombie-skeeter-creatures."

His brother plopped his arms across his chest and frowned. "Why are you always the leader?"

With a chuckle, Mican answered. "Because I'm older, taller, and can see farther."

In disgust, Ashton dropped his arms to his side. "Big stinkin' deal," but he fell in line, following behind Shayla.

They walked through the trees, but continued to scratch their itchy bumps.

Minutes later, Mican stopped and peered into the distance while clawing at his bites. "Can anyone see the water?"

Ashton leaned around his sister. "Not me, I'm at the rear, Oh Mighty Tall One."

"Me either. All I can see is your back," said Shayla with a laugh.

"Okay, let's keep walking."

All of a sudden, Shayla stopped. Ashton stepped on her heels, but she didn't complain. Instead, she spoke in an eerie tone, "Bubbas! Do you hear that?"

Mican turned to her. "What is it Shay-belle?"

She placed her finger to her lips and lowered her voice even more. "Listen! Do you hear voices?"

Ashton shouted, "Holy guacamole! Are they sayin'my name? It sounds like they're sayin' 'get Ashhhh-tonnn.'"

Shayla grabbed him by the arm. "Run, Ashy, come on, Mican!"

A few minutes later, Mican yelled, "Hey, this way. I see water."

Several feet more and they raced out from under the drab trees and ended up at the edge of the creek.

Mican glanced upstream and down. "Can anyone see the dove?"

Ashton's chest rose and fell hard with every breath. "No, but, at least I can't hear voices whispering my name anymore. Can either of you?"

His brother placed his hand on Ashton's shoulder. "No dude, I think we got away."

"Me too, Ashy. I think you're safe now." Shayla released her grip on his arm.

He exhaled a big sigh of relief. "Whew, that's good. Thanks Shay-smell."

She wrinkled her lips at him, then shivered. "My clothes are still a little moist." She reached for Mican's arm. "What are we going to do? Something is after Ashy. We all itch, I'm getting cold, and the dove has left us."

Mican placed his arm around her shoulder. "It's not a problem Shay. We will keep walking upstream in the direction we came from. I'm sure we will see the dove, then we can follow him until we find a way to cross the creek."

She nodded. "Okay. That makes sense," though she still clung to him.

As they walked along, they were flanked by the babbling creek on one side and the dim forest on the other.

Shayla's body began to relax, but that came to a sudden halt when Ashton pointed to the horizon. "Hey guys, look. The sun is startin' to go down. It's gonna be really dark soon."

Tears filled her eyes, then she froze and lowered her voice. "Bubbas, I have a feeling we're being watched again."

They jerked their heads toward the woods and peered deep into the menacing forest.

Ashton whispered, "Is it the skeeter-creatures coming back? Or the creepy voice people?"

His sister squinted, her mouth flew open, but nothing came out. She jumped behind Mican and pointed to the tree line.

Mican and Ashton looked in that direction and narrowed their eyes, staring deep into the woods. Mican asked, "What do you see, Shay?"

It took a second for his eyes to adjust to the dim light before he saw it. The outline of a dragon came into focus. His and Ashton's jaws dropped at almost the same second.

The dragon hesitated, then began to work its way out of its hiding place. Amid the crackling and popping of twigs and underbrush, it moved toward them.

With the dragon almost out of the woods, Ashton realized it kept its long serpent-like neck low to the ground. His mouth got dry, but he managed to utter, "Man, if it stood up straight, that thing would be taller than our house."

The gigantic muscles of its body and legs were clearly visible. Humps, like shoulder blades, stuck up behind its neck, then flattened-out to extend the length of its long body. An awful smell caused their lips and noses to crinkle.

Ashton asked, "Do you guys smell something like," he sniffed the air again. "Like burnt marshmallows, something that was once sweet, but's now ruined?"

As the dragon leaned his face closer, Mican moved to the side, pushing Shayla back with him. "Stay away from us. Please don't come any closer."

They backed away until they came to a place where they could move no further.

Ashton glanced over his shoulder. "Guys, we're up against a gigantic boulder. What're we gonna do?"

The dragon spoke with a gruff, but calm voice. “Are you lost? Do you need help?”

Mican’s voice quivered. “No. We. We just need to go home.”

The creature softened his voice even more. “It seems like you are having trouble finding your way out of the garden. I’m simply asking if you need help.”

Ashton’s back straightened as he blurted out, “If you think we’re having trouble finding our way out of the garden, you must’ve been following us.” His voice rose even more. “Were you following us?”

“Not on purpose, I assure you. I was out for my afternoon stroll and I couldn’t help but notice you. You looked lost, so I thought I would try to help. That’s all.”

Mican edged his way around the stone cliff pulling Shayla with him. “We have to go now. Please leave us alone.”

“Oh, don’t be afraid, children. I live in this garden. I’ve lived here for eons. If you need a guide, I would be glad to help you.”

Shayla tiptoed to reach Mican's ear. "He seems friendly, bubba."

He leaned to the side and lowered his voice. "I don't know, Shay."

Ashton heard him and snapped. "Well, what are we gonna do? Stay here all night? At least let him show us the way outta here."

As the dragon lowered his chin almost to the ground and shifted his head from one sibling to the other, Shayla caught a glimpse of something flickering down his neck. "What is that sparkling on your body?"

The dragon lifted his head. His breath floated over them. "Those are my gemstones. Would you like to look at them more closely?"

Shayla slipped out from behind Mican. He reached for her, but he seemed to be moving in slow motion.

Shayla's arms fell limp at her sides. She slid her feet along, slipping closer to the dragon.

He breathed softly on her again. "Would you like to see the gold and diamonds on my tail too?"

He swished his tail forward, it looped around her legs. The dragon's warm breath swirled over their faces.

She stared at the gems on the dragon's deep jade-green, leathery hide. "Your jewels are very pretty." When the gems and gold shimmered in the fading light, she fell completely under his spell and gasped. "You're so beautiful!"

His bewitching voice drifted over her, as Ashton and Mican watched helplessly. "Little girl, it is getting late. It will be cold soon and your clothes are damp. Why don't you and your brothers come with me. Let me provide safe, warm shelter for you tonight?"

At that moment, Mican broke free from his invisible bonds. "I think we need to go home." He grabbed her arm and snatched her back. "Come on Shay."

The dragon twisted his head a bit, which caused his eyes to sparkle. "Don't you care about your sister and brother? Do you want them to catch their deaths of cold?"

Mican's body stiffened. "Well, of course not."

Bearing his teeth in a grin, the dragon said, "Then why don't you allow me to provide safe, warm shelter for you tonight? You couldn't find your way out of the garden in the bright of day and the light is very dim now." He cleared his throat, adding, "Oh, and if you think you will sleep here on the hillside, you should be aware, there are dangerous creatures who come out after dark, to find their evening meals."

Mican remained defiant. "We will stay right here until someone finds us."

Bowing his head, the dragon backed away. "As you wish." Without another word, he turned to crunch and crash his way into the forest.

A long exhale of breath, betrayed Mican's fear. "Whew! I think we've given the dragon enough time to leave. Let's try to find the path to the gate and get out of this awful place. We need to get home, Mom will be worried sick."

They walked down a slope in their search for a way out of the garden. Finally, they happened upon a flat place with dry, crunchy grass. A few trees were scattered around, the night had grown quite dark, but fireflies came out and appeared to be lighting their way.

Mican stopped for a moment, tipping his head to listen. "Is that the wind, or is that those voices again?"

Ashton said, "Oh no! It sounds like the voices. I think they are sayin 'Get 'emmm. Get 'emmm.' Run guys!"

Dashing past the trees, they soon found a smooth path beneath their feet and slowed their pace. Thankfully, they could no longer hear the hideous voices.

Mican bent over, placed his hands on his knees, panting. "Let's catch our breath, but not for long."

Darkness and silence surrounded them.

After his breathing slowed, Mican spurred them on. "Come on, we need to keep walking." But after only a few steps, trouble struck again.

The ground beneath Shayla's feet crumbled away, her legs slipped into a hole. Her brothers froze. Even in the dim light, they could see her wide eyes and open mouth.

"Help me, boys. Help me!"

They tried to pull her out gently, but she screamed. "Something is biting at my shoe. Hurry. Don't let it eat me! Pull harder!"

Chapter 4

Ohmagosh!

Ashton stepped in closer to grab Shayla's arm, but his weight caused more earth to give way. His foot dropped into the hole next to hers. When he struggled to pull it out, the ground around his sister collapsed. It swallowed her whole—body, head, and long curly hair.

Stunned, Mican and Ashton listened to her muffled voice. "Stop it! Get back! Leave me alone!"

Mican laid on the ground in front of the hole. "Ash, hold my legs!" He dragged himself forward into the opening until he disappeared up to his waist. "I have her, Ash! Pull us out."

Ashton jumped to his feet, grabbed his brother

by the waistband, dragging him back until his body lay above ground, then he tumbled to his knees at the edge of the hole. He reached in, grabbed his sister by the wrists, then struggled to his feet. With one big tug, her head and arms were at the top of the hole.

Mican scrambled to a seated position, gripping Shayla under the arms. Together with a big yank, they pulled her up. She popped from the opening like a cork out of a bottle; and she landed on the ground, trembling between her brothers. But more danger followed.

Right on her heels, a snarling, angry, wicked-looking weasel scurried from the hole. His teeth gleamed in the moonlight.

They jolted backwards.

Shayla gasped and pulled her knees to her chest.

The weasel shook its furry paw at them. “You entered my tunnel without an invitation, you destroyed my home and ruined my dinner.”

Mican jumped to his feet, pulling her up with them. As they backed away, she apologized. “I didn't mean to. It was dark." The pitch of her voice rose. "And I didn't see the hole, then I fell in." Now she yelled, "And I'm sorry! Okay?"

The weasel slunk toward them.

Ashton reached for a sturdy stick to drive it away, but when he bent over to pick it up, the head of a snake rose out of the grass. A pair of glassy eyes stared at him.

Shayla screamed and tried to run. Mican caught her around the waist and lifted her off the ground. Her feet peddled in the air.

"Be still. Don't run," Mican whispered.

She went limp, held captive by her brother.

Ashton tried to move away from the snake, but stumbled and crashed into a mountainous anthill.

Two-inch-long ants rushed to the surface and swarmed his body in seconds. From head to toe they assaulted him. "Oh my gosh, Ow! Help me get up. I need to run."

With every bite, the pain stabbed, like electric shocks filled with hot toxin. The bites covered his face, back, arms, and legs. He bellowed in pain.

"Ouch. Sheesh, Mican, help me."

His brother dropped Shayla with a *plunk* and grabbed a branch. "Here Ash, take hold of this."

All Ashton could do was to slap at his body.

Mican tried again. "Ash, grab it."

Shayla cupped her hands around her mouth. "Grab the branch, Ashy. Try!"

Ashton tried, but the branch broke.

Finally, he rolled from the anthill, ants followed him, spreading toward Mican and Shayla.

"Ash, get up! I have to save Shay." Mican grabbed his sister by the arm and ran back the way they had come. They passed the weasel who now stood on his hind legs. As Mican pulled Shayla along, her feet only struck the ground with every third step he took. He towed her behind him, like a kite he wanted to get airborne.

By the time Ashton scrambled to his feet, he ran to follow his brother and sister, but darkness prevented him. He couldn't tell which way they'd gone. When he stopped to catch his breath, he found himself alone, under a big tree. Eerie voices seeped down through the branches.

He froze, listening, then in a panic, he dashed into the darkness. Wandering, cold and afraid, he staggered onto a path. After a minute, he spotted a faint halo of light. In its frame, stood his brother and sister. As he approached, their voices drifted toward him. He slowed his pace to listen.

Shayla stared at the ground, sobbing. "We need to go back for Ashy. We shouldn't have left him."

"I had no choice, Shay." Mican placed his hands on his knees. "Ash couldn't hold onto the branch. I tried to help him. You saw me. We will have to wait here for him to catch up."

Tears filled her eyes, she stomped her foot. "We shouldn't have left him."

Mican pulled her closer. "Are you hurt?"

She breathed heavily. "No, only scrapes and scratches I think." Trembling, she said, "I'm sorry. I know you tried to help Ashy, but we shouldn't have left him."

"I couldn't think of anything else to do. I had to save you."

"Thank you for thinking of me and for pulling me out of that horrible hole. I was so scared. I could feel something tickling my skin. It felt like spider webs. For a minute, I thought I might be spun into a cocoon, but then when I fell all the way in, I knew something else was in there with me. It was too dark to see what it was, but I could hear it breathing."

"What were you afraid of, Shay?" He jumped at her and growled. "Afffrrraid something was going to eat you?" And he laughed.

She stared at the ground and tears slipped down her cheeks. "No, I was afraid I was never going to see Momma again."

The smile faded from Mican's face, but he managed to say, "Awww, Shay-belle. You know I wasn't going to let that happen."

She flung herself at him and wrapped her arms around his middle.

After a brief moment, their hug came to an end when they heard Ashton. He walked up to them groaning. "Ouch. Man. Ow. Sheesh." He continued to scratch, but shouted, "You cowards, you left me!"

"Ash, I tried to help, but I had to get Shayla out of there."

A stone-cold look shot from his eyes. "I heard what you said. That's right, save your Shay-belle. Let me die."

Shayla wept. "Ashy, I'm sorry. Please forgive us."

"As usual, I had to take care of myself. Man, those guys can really bite. It felt like they had needles for teeth. Now on top of the mosquito bites, which had almost stopped itching, I've got these ant bites. At first, they stung like a blast of fire, but now they itch something fierce."

While her brothers glared at each other, Shayla shivered. "Ashy, are you going to be all right?"

"I guess so, but I'm massively itchy." He lifted one pant leg, crushing an ant, as he scratched a big bite. He held out the dead ant. "Look at these demon-ants! They're as big as Shayla's little finger. Then he looked up. "Oh yeah, I heard those creepy-sounding voices again."

Shayla hugged her shoulders, shivering. "What did they say, Ashy?"

"They said, 'If we can stop those three, the Keystone kids will never know.'"

Mican curved his hand over his chin and mouth. "Hmmm. I guess we are the three, but who are the Keystone kids? I remember an old movie about Keystone Cops, but who are their kids?"

Ashton continued to scratch his itches. "I don't know, but since you read so much, I figured you might."

"I have no idea," said Mican.

In the pale light, Shayla glanced down at her arms, then at her brothers. She held hers in front of her. "Look, bubbas. Our mosquito bites are beginning to sink in. They look like little dents, or little bellybuttons, all over our arms and faces. I wonder how much blood those mosquitoes sucked out?"

Ashton stopped scratching. He stared at his sister. "I wonder if they were carrying the West Nile or Zika virus? Or that new ones, Triple E? That one is even more deadly."

Shayla drew her arms around her body. "Oooo, that's not good. I hadn't thought about that."

Ashton wrinkled his brows and changed his tone. "Can someone scratch my back?"

Shayla stepped behind him, placed her fingertips on his back, gently brushing from side-to-side. "Wow, Ashy, I can feel the bumps through your shirt. You're covered."

He sighed a long heavy breath. "Ahhhh, that feels so good. Thanks, Shay." He chuckled. "Lucky for me, it turned out the weasel and the snake had unfinished business. I had my hands full with those ants." As he straightened, he gazed into the distance.

"What's up, Ash? You look weird. Your eyes look glazed over. Are you in shock?"

Ignoring his brother, Ashton stared along the path behind Mican. "Look guys, I think I see the source of this light. In fact, that's how I found you. In the dark, you were framed by a faint glow."

Shayla leaned to the side and looked around her brothers. "Maybe someone lives in the garden to take care of it. Maybe they can help us."

With a firm voice, Ashton announced, "Let's chance it. I'm miserable. My clothes are damp. I'm cold and these ant bites itch like mad. Let's check it out."

Mican watched his brother clawing at his arms. "Stop scratching, Ash. You're making me itchy again."

"Duhhhh, yeah right. I'll stop scratching, just for you, bruh."

Ashton pushed his brother aside and took the lead. Halfway down the path, he crouched low, to sneak along the trail. His brother and sister did the same.

Being bent over allowed Mican to examine the walkway. "This path is made of pebbles, but they've been pressed deep into the dirt. It feels like a cobblestone road, but made with much smaller rocks. I wonder what could have mashed them into the ground like this?"

Instead of answering the question, Ashton said, "The wind is chilly and I smell smoke, maybe there's a fire where I can at least get warm."

They crept closer to the light and rounded a bend, there they found good news and bad news.

The good news—the light reflected from a roaring campfire. The bad news—they discovered what mashed the pebbles into the ground.

Behind the flames, sat the dragon, quietly poking the fire with a stick. He didn't lift his eyes, but his voice boomed. "Oh, I see you found me. Good. I've been waiting here for you, in case you changed your minds."

No one spoke for a moment, until Mican said, "We saw the light from your fire and …."

The dragon looked up and softened his voice. "Why don't you come closer and dry yourselves. I can see from here that the little girl is shivering." He wagged his head. "The poor little thing needs to get warm. We can sit here for a few minutes." He looked over his shoulder. "My home is over there. You can join me; you will be safe and comfortable for the night."

Around the fire, tall boulders stood in a semi-circle. The bank of rocks reflected the light and the heat. In front of the curved wall, other stones had been stacked like a bench. It made a perfect place to dry their clothes and to warm their bodies.

Mican took off his shoes and socks. He placed them on the rocks close to the fire.

Ashton and Shayla followed his example.

Stepping between the rock-sofa and the fire, Mican eased himself onto the warm bench.

His sister came in next to him, while Ashton sat on the outside edge. Their feet rested in the warm grass. It pushed up around their ankles, giving their feet a welcoming hug.

Shayla untied her sweater and spread it on a large rock in front of her.

Their bodies began to relax in the comforting warmth, except for Ashton, who rubbed his back against the rock behind him to scratch his savage itches.

His sister reached over and pushed him forward.

"Ashy, you need to stop scratching. Your back is bleeding."

"I can't help it, Shay. These bites itch something awful."

The fire crackled, snapped, and flickered in front of them. Tiny red sparks rose on the hot air.

Ashton's stomach began to growl. "Now if we only had some hotdogs."

Shayla gave him another shove. "Oh, Ashy."

"I can't help it, I'm hungry."

Mican sat speechless. His hands clamped together in front of him.

The dragon noticed his movements and asked in a gruff, but friendly voice, "Well, boy, will you and your brother and sister be joining me tonight, or do you prefer to go wandering again?"

He glanced at Ashton and Shayla. "Do either of you have any ideas?"

They gazed at him and wagged their heads *no.*

Ashton and Shayla stared into the fire while Mican replied. "I can't think of any other answer, so yes, I guess we will accept your—uh—invitation to spend the night."

"Wonderful!" shouted the dragon. "Please gather your belongings."

It took a couple of minutes for them to put on their socks and shoes.

Shayla tied her warm, dry sweater around her waist, and the dragon led them to a mountain of rocks behind the fire ring.

When they drew close, an opening between two towering boulders lay before them.

Ashton gave a soft chuckle. "We don't have to worry about whether we'll fit through there or not."

As the dragon led them through the entryway, they waded into pitch-black darkness.

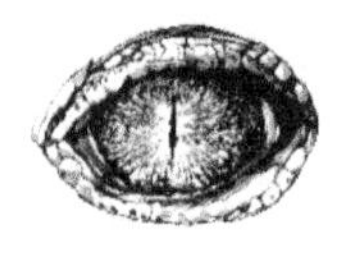

Chapter 5

The Dragon's Den

Inside the cave, they couldn't see a thing, but they could hear water trickling somewhere in the distance.

Mican's voice came out shaky. "Where are we?" He cleared his throat and tried again. "Tell us where we are!"

Shayla stretched her arms out in front of her to find her brother. When she touched him, she grabbed hold of his shirt. "Mican, I'm scared."

"Just stay close to me, Shay."

"Thanks, bubba. Ashy, are you here too?"

"Right behind you, I think."

Little-by-little, their eyes adjusted to the darkness. Ashton noticed a pale light growing in the distance. “Hey guys, back there. It looks like there’s some sorta drop-off and some kinda light is reflecting up the wall, into the cave.”

All at once, a foul odor pushed past them. Shayla held onto Mican’s shirt with one hand, but with the other, she fanned in front of her face. “What is that smell? It’s awful. It smells like rotten eggs.”

As the scent filled their nostrils, Mican answered. “I think that’s the smell of sulfur.”

Shayla turned loose of her brother’s shirt and pinched her nose. The other arm hugged her body. “It stinks in here and it feels cold after getting warm by the fire.”

Without warning, a blast of air erupted the cave. A flash of light forced them to squint. Nearby a pile of twigs burst into flames.

Shayla jumped. “How’d that happen?”

They now watched as the dragon tilted his head toward them, baring his sharp teeth. “How do you think a dragon lights a fire, silly girl?”

The fire blazed brighter and drowned out the

distant light. The stink of sulfur mixed with the damp, musty smell of the cave. The new light revealed the jagged, gray ceiling and rough stone walls of the huge cavern.

Ashton scanned the vast expanse. “Dude, you could put a two-story house in here.”

The floor felt flat and smooth, but not always level. The ceiling had string-like tentacles hanging from it.

Mican tapped Shayla and pointed. “Those must be roots from plants above this place. They look kind of like spiderwebs. That must be what you felt in the weasel’s hole.”

Ashton stared at a dark substance flowing across the path near the back of the room.

Watching him gaze toward the stream, the dragon made an offer. “You can go take a drink if you are thirsty, the water is fresh; if you splash your face and arms, your bites will quieten down.”

The muscles around Ashton’s eyes tightened. “Is that part of the same stream we played in earlier today? Will we be attacked by piranha?” His eyes darted back toward the dragon.

"There are no piranhas in here, not inside my den." His gruff voice softened with a hint of kindness. "You are free to drink and wash without any worries; please be my guests, make yourselves at home."

Squirming inside his shirt from the fierce itching, Ashton looked toward the stream of blackness that flowed across the distant rock. He made a move to step past his brother and sister.

Mican tried to stop him. "Ash, what are you doing?"

"I'm accepting our host's offer of something to drink, I'm thirsty. And besides, my bites still itch like wildfire. I want to see if the water really works."

Shayla's voice trembled. "Be careful, Ashy."

"I'm okay, Shay, don't worry. We are guests and we have been told to make ourselves at home."

Spotting a pile of bones heaped up at the far side, Shayla timidly glanced toward the dragon. "Mr. Dragon, are you going to cook us and eat us?"

The dragon laughed. "No, silly girl. I only use fire when it is needed for the comforts of life." He tucked his chin. "Like warming a cold, dark cave for visitors."

Ashton now spotted the bone pile and pointed. "Then where did those come from?"

The dragon's eyes sparkled in the firelight, a gentle curl of smoke escaped from his nostrils. "Don't worry children. I only eat wild animals and uncooked ones at that."

Shayla and Ashton both exhaled a sigh of relief.

When he reached the edge of the stream, Ashton turned to face his siblings. "Hey, guys. From back there, this looked like ink, but when you get up to it, it's just water."

He lowered himself onto one knee, bent to take a drink, lifted a double handful of water to his mouth and slurped it in. "Ahhhh, that is good. I was so thirsty."

Some of the water dribbled down the front of his shirt. "Man, that feels good."

He splashed water onto his face and allowed it

to run down his neck. “Wow, this actually works. Where the water washed over my bites, it feels so much better.” He dipped his arms in the water, then stood. As he walked back to his brother and sister, he turned his attention to another matter. “I have another question. If you don’t mind.”

“Yes, what is it?”

“If you’re not gonna eat us, do you have anything we can eat?” He gave a few light pats to his stomach. “I’m really hungry.”

Mican stuck his hands out to the side. “Seriously, Ash? I doubt dragons eat the same things people do.”

The dragon paused for a moment, tapping his chin with a sharp, curved claw. “Hmm, let me see.” He stuck his large paw into a recess in the wall and pulled out some dried fruits and berries. He shoved his hand toward Ashton and opened it. “Will these do?”

When he stepped forward, Mican threw up his hands. “Ash, think about it.” He paused. “How do you know they’re not poisoned?”

The dragon flung his head back and exploded into laughter that echoed deep into the cave. He glared at Mican. “What are you thinking, boy? Do you think you are in a fairytale?” He lowered his head closer to Mican’s face, the skin over one eye crept up. “I’m simply trying to share a few bites of food with my guests.” He glanced toward Ashton and raised the stiff hide over the other eye. “But I can eat them myself if you don’t want ….”

Ashton lunged forward. “No, I will take some.” He grabbed a handful of berries, but accidentally scratched his wrist on a claw. “Ouch!”

“Oh, I’m sorry, boy. Dip the wound in the stream, it will be fine.”

Shayla stared at Mican, her eyes resembled puppy-dog eyes, her chin trembled. “I’m hungry too.”

Mican lifted his arms at his sides, then dropped them. “Okay, Ash, give it a little taste.”

But instead, Ashton took a big bite.

His brother rolled his eyes. “So much for a little taste, Ash.”

Ashton sputtered a mist of juice as he tried to talk with his mouth full. "Wow, these are great. Best berries I've ever tasted."

Shayla cast a glance at the berries, then at Mican. He gave her a nod. They walked over and lifted their hands toward the dragon's outstretched claw. Each got a handful of food and Mican took a small bite.

"Hmm, you're right, Ash. These do taste great."

Ashton laughed so hard, he accidentally spattered dots of juice everywhere, then he swallowed with a big gulp. "Man, I don't hear that very often."

Lifting a berry to her mouth, Shayla tilted her head to the side. "Don't hear what very often, Ashy?"

"One of you actually said I was right about something." He laughed again.

After they'd filled their bellies, the dragon directed them to walk toward the back of the chamber. "Go get a drink, and clean yourselves up for the night. You have sticky juice all over you.

And you, little girl, you have muddy streaks on your face and arms."

Shayla frowned, but turned to join her brothers as they walked toward the rear of the cave. They reached the flowing water and knelt beside it.

Mican suggested, "To keep from stirring the water too much, let's each take turns getting a drink. Ash, you go first since you have already washed some. Shay, because your hands are so dirty, will you wait till last, if that's okay?"

She stared at her arms and hands before nodding.

Mican and Ashton drank until satisfied.

Shayla's turn came, she knelt to wash her hands and face, after the dirty water rushed away, she drank. All of a sudden, she noticed the strangest thing happen. "Bubbas, when the water touched the mosquito-dents, they popped back to normal, some kind of thorn-looking-thingy dropped out and floated away."

Ashton sat down next to her. "When I washed the first time, it felt so good, I didn't notice what happened to my dents." He proceeded to take off his shoes and socks, then pulled up his pants. He stretched his legs out into the water and splashed the wounds. He took off his shirt and tried to scoop water to pour down his back, but most of it dribbled out before he could raise his hands over his head.

Shayla got to her knees. "I see what you are trying to do. Let me help."

As she poured handfuls of water down his back, she gasped. "Ashy, all of the bites and bloody streaks are disappearing. It looks like the blood is being sipped away through tiny, invisible straws and then vanishes. And the bites are flattening out like they're being ironed. I wish you could see this."

"That's okay, Shay. I can feel it. That's what matters."

Ashton felt so much better, he stretched out on the cave floor with his feet and legs still in the water. His arms relaxed at his sides for the first time since his battle with the ants. The water splashed onto him, then slipped around and under his legs with a gurgling sound. He lifted his hand to examine the scratch for infection. "Hey guys. That nasty scratch on my wrist is gone. All I can see is a faint, white line where it used to be."

The water swept away the musty smell of the cave, as it rushed by it left the air fresh around the stream. Ashton lay there with a smile on his face. "Wow, this feels good. What a relief."

While Ashton lay on the floor, he noticed Mican glance back toward the cave entrance. He pushed up onto his elbow. Darkness filled the opening. They had no choice now, but to stay.

The dragon lowered his head and addressed his guests. "You all look exhausted." His front leg swished to the right in a grand gesture. "Come. Lie down on this bed of dried leaves that I prepared for you earlier today."

They made their way toward the front of the cavern. Ashton, being very tired from their adventures, made the mistake of asking, "Are you gonna eat us in our sleep, now that we've eaten your fruit and berries?"

The dragon's head drew back and he belted out

a growl. Dust drifted from the ceiling. He narrowed his eyes and bellowed, "Look, child."

Ashton felt insulted by being called a child, after all, he was twelve.

But the dragon continued, "If I had meant to eat you, boy, you would have been eaten by now. Do you understand?"

Shayla tried to calm him. "Mr. Dragon, I want to thank you for your help and for the delicious food. Can I ask you your name? What would you like for us to call you?"

Clearing his throat, he softened his tone. "Little girl, I am known by many names, but you can call me Friend. Now that is enough for tonight. It is time to go to sleep. We will talk more tomorrow, and I will show you the way to the gate."

Mican felt a tug on his sleeve. Shayla cupped her hand to her mouth. Mican bent to meet her. After she whispered in his ear, he stood straight and addressed the dragon. "Excuse me."

Again, a burst of anger erupted from the dragon with a roar. "What is it now?"

"Uhhh, my sister, uhhh, needs to—you know."

"What is it, boy? Spit it out."

"Uhhh, where is your bathroom?"

"I normally go outside."

Shayla glanced toward the entrance. She shivered and whimpered. "But it's dark outside."

"Hmmmm, I guess you will have to go in here then."

"But." She stopped.

"But what?" burst the dragon.

"But everyone will be able to see me."

A second puff of smoke curled from his nostrils, but this time darker. "Well, find a spot in the shadows, past the bone pile."

She turned. The further she walked toward the darkness, the rougher the floor became. She wrinkled her nose as she passed the stinky pile of bones. "He could at least throw those worthless things outside." She stopped in the edge of the shadow. "Can you still see me?"

"That's fine, Shay. Now hurry."

She soon stepped back into the light and crossed

over to the stream to wash her hands again. Returning to the leaf-bed, Shayla nodded to the dragon. "Thank you."

Ashton pressed his lips together and squirmed. "Y'know, now that I think about it."

Mican sighed. "Okay, make it quick. When you get back, I'll go."

After everyone had relieved themselves, Shayla untied her sweater and stepped onto the bed of leaves. Lying down, she spread her sweater over her arms and shoulders like a blanket.

The dragon scanned the bedding area as the boys rolled down their shirt sleeves and stretched out on either side of her. Even though tiredness covered him, Ashton figured he wouldn't be able to sleep a wink.

On the opposite side of the chamber, the dragon curled up next to the stone wall. Clearly, he had lain there many nights because the wall had been worn smooth in that spot. The dragon surprised them when he began to sing a strange and haunting melody. The crackle of the fire tossed red embers into the air and the light flickered all around.

Shayla whispered, “Look how the flames dance against the walls and ceiling when he sings.”

The song and the flickering light, made them dizzy. The dizziness made them feel like the leaf-bed began to spin, like a merry-go-round. The illusion of the bed revolving, had the effect of a sleeping potion.

Against his will, Ashton’s eyelids became heavy and slid shut.

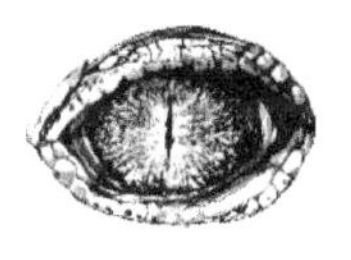

Chapter 6

The Next Morning

When Ashton awoke, the fire had died down to ashes, and a small amount of light seeped through the entrance of the cave. He raised up on one elbow to check on his brother and sister. They seemed fine, so he sat up. He couldn't see the dragon, so he reached across Shayla to wake Mican.

Mican jumped.

As Ashton woke Shayla, he lifted his finger to his lips. "Shhhh, come on. Get up."

They rose as quietly as anyone could on dried leaves and twigs.

Shayla twisted up her lips as she picked a few leaves out of her mass of curls and dropped them back onto the bed.

Mican led the way as they crept toward the mouth of the cave, his sister and brother followed.

As they emerged from the darkness, the booming voice of the dragon greeted them. “Good morning, guests. I hope you slept well.”

Slightly shaken, they each, in turn said, “Yes, good morning,” with Shayla adding “Friend,” to her reply.

The light in the area appeared dim and murky, but they could see the dragon smile. “Let’s go find that gate, shall we?” He turned and began to trudge through the bushes, making a wide path with his body and tail.

Shayla smiled. “Thank you for showing us the way to the gate.”

The dragon nodded. “Certainly, little girl, but first let’s stop and eat some wild grapes. You must be hungry again. I know I am.”

Ashton rubbed his belly and smiled. “I could use a little nibble of something, now that you mention it.”

A vine of ripe grapes hung across some bushes

next to the new path; purple and juicy, they hung low enough for Shayla to reach.

Mican wagged his head. "Well hurry up, you two. We really need to go home."

Ashton twisted and stretched in delight. "Man, it feels good not to have all of those bites and itches."

Shayla munched and nodded with a smile.

Even Mican gave in and took part in the fruity breakfast, but when he decided they had, had enough, he announced. "Time for us to go." He turned to the dragon. "Please take us to the gate now."

The dragon wiped his mouth and smiled. "I will, but I want to show you a lovely waterfall that's on the way."

Mican shook his head. "No thank you. We need to get home. Our mom will be worried."

Pulling his head back, the dragon tucked his chin. "Nonsense, if she has not come looking for you by now, you are not missed."

Ashton tightened his muscles and balled his hands into fists. "That's not true. She just doesn't know where we are."

The dragon tipped his head to the side. "What kind of mother doesn't know where her children are?"

Shayla looked to the ground, her bottom lip rolled out. "I thought you said you were our friend."

"Oh, little girl, I'm so sorry to hurt your feelings, but you must know it's true."

One tear leaked from Shayla's eye.

Mican spotted his sister's downcast face and shouted at the dragon. "Leave my sister alone. We have a wonderful mother who loves us very much."

Rather than answering Mican, the dragon turned to Ashton. "Is that true, little boy?"

But before Ashton could speak, Mican shouted. "Of course, it's true."

The dragon asked Ashton another question. "Does your brother always speak for you?"

Ashton glared at Mican and tightened his mouth. "He tries, but no, actually he doesn't speak for me. I can speak for myself."

They walked along in silence, until they entered

a clearing on the edge of a river, there, a warm breeze greeted them.

The dragon paused. “Look up ahead, children. Isn’t that the most beautiful sight you have ever seen?”

A fluffy cloud of mist floated above the top of a large, waterfall. The water flowed gracefully over a flat stone and crashed into the river below.

With their mouths slightly open, they walked toward the scene. A sweetness, like a natural perfume rode on the breeze.

Shayla shouted, “The air tastes like honeysuckles.”

They took a few steps closer to the lovely falling water. The sight, the smell, and the coolness crowded their senses, as they admired the grand view. Green vines, dotted with white flowers and wet with spray, glistened in the sunlight.

Shayla stared at the beautiful scene.

With a gleam in his eyes, the dragon smirked. “No little girl, you are not dreaming.”

Her eyes flashed up sharply. “How did you

know what I was thinking?"

"Oh, your face said it all, little girl."

Mican broke in, "Okay, the waterfall is great, but we have to get home. I'm sure our mom is searching for us."

Ignoring him, the dragon stepped off the bank and under the cascading water. "I need to take a shower first. I don't want to hurt your feelings, but you three could use some freshening up too."

Mican straightened his back and shouted. "No. No more delays. Show us the way to the gate."

The dragon stepped out from under the waterfall and gave a mighty shake; water went everywhere, including splashing onto them. Ashton assumed the dragon was about to agree, but instead he defiantly lifted his chin. "If that is the way you want to be, find it yourselves." He wheeled around to stomp his way back into the woods.

Shayla dashed forward. "No, wait. Come back."

Mican shouted, "Let him go, Shay. We can find our own way out." He led the way, but they ended up rambling for hours looking for the gate, or for the dove, or for someone to help them, but no help could be found. No matter where they turned, more tall trees or lush green garden stretched out before them.

Deep in thought, Ashton's eyes glazed over, suddenly he announced. "Mican, this cannot be true. How can a garden this big be in the woods behind our house without us knowing about it? But here we are, as impossible as it seems."

For the first time, Mican shared his true feeling. "Ash, I'm really beginning to worry."

"I'm scared," said Shayla, "and hungry again."

Ashton took that moment to vent his anger at her. "This is all your fault, Shay. You pushed past us and ran into the garden. And it was you that wanted to follow the stupid fish. That turned out to be a great idea, didn't it?"

Mican exploded. "Stop it, Ash. Leave her alone. We all decided to follow the dove."

"Go ahead, defend your *belle*. She's as dumb as one. *Dumbbell,* get it?"

"I call her belle because she's pretty. You know

that and you know she's not dumb."

Ashton smirked. "Shay-belle makes her sound like she's a cat. Here, kitty! Here Shay-belle."

At that moment, the dragon shuffled back into view. "Well, well, well. Who have we here? Haven't you three found your way home yet?"

Ashton wheeled around and stared at the dragon. His face burned. "No, as you can plainly see."

The dragon stretched his neck and smiled. "Looks like I will have guests again tonight."

Mican pushed his shoulders back. "No way, not this time. You are trying to keep us here. I know it."

Jerking his head to the side. "Okay, as you wish. Sleep outside in the cold night air. It will teach you to appreciate a warm bed when it's offered."

Shayla grabbed Mican's arm and looked up at him. "Wait. Shouldn't we go with him? Remember all the creatures that attacked us?"

"No Shay, he has lied to us and delayed us long enough."

The dragon whipped his head toward them. A

burst of dark smoke blasted from his nostrils. “Lied to you. Delayed you. Is that the thanks I get for giving you food and shelter?”

“Yes. You said you’d show us the way out of the garden, but you haven’t. All you’ve done is delay us.” Mican folded his arms across his chest.

The dragon softened his voice. “I thought you might like to see the sights on your way, but then you insulted me. I left you to find your own way; you didn’t do a very good job of it, did you?” The dragon grinned.

Mican leaned forward and punched his fists toward the ground. “You showed us the waterfall to keep us here. I’m sure of it.”

The dragon threw his head high and puffed out his chest. “I rule this garden. You have no right to talk to me that way. I’ve been blamed long enough.” He snapped his large tail like a whip, and in a flash, he wrapped it around the middle of Ashton’s body, pinning his arms to his sides. The dragon gripped him and stomped away.

Mican and Shayla ran alongside the dragon,

pounding on his powerful legs.

Shayla screamed. “Stop. Let my brother go!”

No matter how hard they tried, they were unable to stop him.

The dragon trotted, then ran.

Mican chased him with Shayla trailing behind, but when he reached the edge of a cliff, the dragon leapt into the air and spread an enormous pair of wings. He disappeared into a deep ravine, but with one powerful push of his wings, he rocketed into the sky. His jade green scales and the jewels on his back and tail reflected the reddening sunlight.

Mican and Shayla had no choice but to stop at the edge of the cliff.

The last thing Ashton heard was Shayla’s voice. “Ashy’s head and legs are flopping around like a rag doll. And it’s all my fault.”

As her words faded away, Ashton saw Mican’s hand reach for his cell phone, but from his reaction, it was safe to assume the light flashed, *No service.*

***

The dragon soared in a furious manner. It only took a minute for him to reach his lair, he roared and spewed smoke all the way.

When they arrived at the cliff, the dragon's wings folded in, he plopped down and skidded to a hard, rough landing outside the cave.

Ashton's feet thumped the ground, it jarred him to the core, his teeth banged together, pain shot up through his mouth. "Ow!" The beast stormed through the narrow entrance. His body and tail swished with such force, Ashton yelled, "Dude, don't smash me against the rocks."

As the dragon disappeared through the entryway, Ashton disappeared into darkness.

Inside the cave, the dragon snapped his tail and flung Ashton onto the cold, stone floor. He landed on his right shoulder, then tumbled toward the far side of the cave. His head hit the stone wall.

Chapter 7

Life or Death

Ashton had no way of knowing how long he had been unconscious, but as he awoke, he heard the dragon puffing and stomping on the other side of the cave.

"Delay them? Wasn't I a good host? Didn't I feed them and tell them of the healing power of the water? Didn't I supply them with a warm, dry place to sleep? Was that a lie? They should be thanking me. They should be praising me. But no. All I get are insults." He roared and flames burst from his mouth, lighting the cavern.

The flash revived Ashton even more from his foggy, dream-like state. As he struggled to become more aware of his surroundings, he became painfully aware of a throbbing lump on his head and an injury to his shoulder. Pushing through the pain, he dragged himself back and tucked his body into a crevice in the wall.

The smell of sulfur and the stuffiness of the cave filled his mouth and nose. His head pounded. With every movement, his shoulder pulsed with pain. To make it even worse, he had backpedaled next to the disgusting bone pile. The sight of the bones made him feel sick, but an idea sprang into his mind.

The dragon glared at him. His scales scraped the floor as he moved toward Ashton. He fumed and growled, and the floor shook. “You cannot hide from me, boy.”

Ashton’s fear rose, but he managed to keep his wits about him. When the dragon had talked to Shayla about the jewels and gold down his back and tail, he had displayed a lot of pride and a high need for respect. Those facts and the bone pile now fueled an idea.

He addressed the dragon and began to apologize. "I'm sorry we hurt your feelings. And I'm sorry my brother insulted you. He can be like that sometimes. I know you deserve to be treated better."

The dragon paused, his neck pulled back and his chin rose. "Yes! That is right."

Ashton believed his plan could work. He continued talking. "Having such beautiful gemstones on your back and sparkling gold and diamonds on your tail, I'm sure you would want to know that even after taking a shower, you have a big splotch of grape juice on your face."

The dragon stared at him, his eyelids squished down.

Ashton's courage rose. "If you come closer, I will show you where it is. I know you would like to wash it off."

As the serpent slowly approached, he bent his neck toward Ashton.

With some difficulty, Ashton managed to get to a squatting position. He reached beside his left foot and grabbed a long bone. Leaning against the cave wall, he slid himself up, snagging his shirt on the rough stone. As he stood, he dragged the bone along behind his leg. At the last second, he sprang up and jammed the bone into the dragon's nose.

When Ashton jumped, a searing pain struck his shoulder. He hugged his right arm to his chest and dashed toward the cave entrance.

Furious and in pain, the dragon roared and the mountain trembled. Dirt drifted from the ceiling. He violently whipped his neck back and forth, loosening the bone from his nose. With a fiery blast, it rocketed toward Ashton like a missile.

Flames washed over him as the bone made contact at the back of his knees, knocking him to the stone floor. He smoked from the scorching and his head ached. The dragon's massive tail slashed across the floor and slapped Ashton like a hockey puck. The impact propelled him at high speed toward the ledge at the rear of the cavern.

When Ashton's eyes opened, flashes of light filled his vision. The flickers reminded him of sparklers burning on the Fourth of July. As his sight cleared, he found himself lying face down, his head dangling over the drop-off at the rear of the cavern and he stared into a pit.

Far below, a lake of steaming liquid swirled, the surface—smooth like red and gold satin.

A strange thought pierced his mind. That was beautiful.

Hot gases rose, striking him in the face, he coughed and snapped back to the moment; the choking fumes threatened to knock him out again. He tried to slide away from the edge, but he couldn't move. A darker thought hit him. Was he paralyzed?

He wiggled his fingers and toes. He could move, but every twitch ignited agony in his shoulder, and now his ribs and legs sent sharp waves of torment to his brain. The pain throbbed unbearably.

Behind him, the dragon roared and spewed threats. Furious from the pain in his nose and from being deceived, he shouted, "Little fool! If you think you will ever escape from me now, you are mistaken. Try to trick me! You will find out what happens to those who try. I will end you, boy."

Ashton lay in a heap on the stone precipice, his head swam from the gases and pain, but he could hear the dragon coming.

As the serpent slithered closer, his scales drug across the stone floor, sounding like sandpaper. With every thud of the dragon's feet, the rock vibrated beneath Ashton's body. Dust stirred with each step the dragon took and filled what little air he had to breathe.

In a split second, sickening thoughts crashed in and filled his mind. Was his time up? Was this the end? The thoughts mixed with flashes of clarity. He had always been jealous of Shayla, but she had always been good to him. Like yesterday, when she helped to scratch his itchy bites and splashed the healing water over his back.

His heart had been as hard as the stone his body now laid on. Just like Mican said, the words he had breathed out were poison, like the air he now breathed in. Shay would never have told him that she wished he had never been born. His former words clawed at his mind and emotions, now she would never know how sorry he was.

Light flickered from the steaming lake below, the gases made him sick. He threw up into the pit, his vomit sizzled as it hit the slowly revolving mass below. That drained most of his remaining strength.

His mind raced. He had always hated having Mican or Shayla with him every minute of every day. Again, like Mican had said, he had his wish. He was now alone. A flood of sadness poured into his brain. If only he could have them here now. He had never had to be by himself before, now he faced death without his family. The depth of his loneliness was equaled only by the depth of the pit he now stared into.

He missed them very much, but was glad they weren't here. He was glad they were safe, but also sad that they would never know his new feelings.

With a deep pang of regret, it became clear to Ashton that his brother had always tried to watch over him, but Mican would never know how grateful he was, or should have been. It dawned on him, he would never be able to tell his family how much he truly loved them.

Like yesterday morning, when Grammy gave him the binoculars for my birthday, she kissed his cheek. Why had he wiped it off? She said he was special and would grow into a fine man, but now this was to be his fate. He would never know what he might have been. She would never know. No one would ever know.

What a sad and pitiful end this was. He was lost.

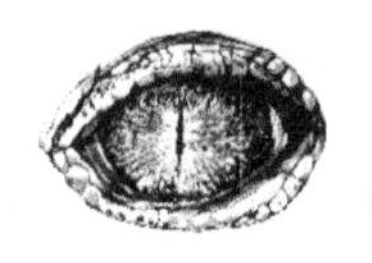

Chapter 8

Call on the King

A light gradually growing brighter captured Ashton's attention, he snapped back to the moment. His eyes rested on an outline of the dove as it came into focus below the edge of the drop off. Surely it couldn't be. His mind must have been playing tricks on him. The dove had left them, but the familiar, small voice broke through. "Ask the King to rescue you. Quickly, Ashton, call on him."

Using his last remaining breath, he cried out. "King, your majesty, please rescue me. Save me and forgive me for all my anger and jealousy."

A blinding streak of lightning flashed across the cavern, followed by a loud *boom* that echoed in the chamber.

A very large man stood on thin air just below the ledge where Ashton lay. The man's muscular arms rippled with power as he drew an enormous golden sword, his legs were like tree trunks braced against the wind. Yet in spite of all of his apparent strength, the man's gentle voice soothed Ashton. "Close your eyes, lad, and do not be afraid."

Ashton squeezed his eyes shut and the tickle of something feathery covered him. Instantly, a fresh breeze replaced the toxic fumes of the abyss. A bed of soft, green grass replaced the cold, stone floor beneath him. The terrible pain in his body was gone. Now able to move, he pushed himself to a sitting position. A noble-looking horse stood protectively beside him, the enormous man stood in front of him; the giant sword now safely tucked into its sheath.

The man stepped forward. "Come, Lad." He lifted Ashton as if he weighed no more than a leaf and placed him on the back of the waiting horse. Before the man turned to leave, he spoke again. "Fear not. The horse's name is Warrior. He will protect you and take you back to your brother and sister." The man took a step to leave and vanished, as if he slipped through a rip in a curtain.

The horse took a step. A dizziness came over Ashton. Had space and time just folded?

His mind cleared, and a few feet away, the huge man stood beside his brother and sister who knelt in the grass next to the ravine.

Shayla wept.

Ashton heard the man's voice. "The King has heard your request. Your brother is safe."

Mican and Shayla stared at the gigantic man.

Shayla wiped her eyes and blinked.

Mican poured out his heart. "I know I could have been nicer to Ash. I did try to leave him out of things. There is no excuse for it, I'm the older brother. I should have been nicer to him. I should have talked to him and asked him why he acted the way he did. I should have done better."

The man replied, "The King forgives you," then he slipped through the curtain again.

At the sound of rustling leaves, Mican and

Shayla faced the forest.

Warrior walked into the open area and came to a halt.

Ashton leaned forward, threw his leg over the horse's rear and slid off. His feet landed gently on the ground.

Mican and Shayla scrambled to their feet and ran to him, with Mican shouting. "Are you okay? How did you get away? Where did you find the horse?"

With both hands, Shayla wiped the tears from her face, as she chased after Mican. "Oh Ashy, I was so worried. I'm so glad to see you. I'm so sorry."

He stood there, his arms hanging limp at his sides and he fought back tears. Wow, could his heart be swelling in his chest? He had never felt like this before. He had never seen such love and concern from his brother and sister. They loved him, they really loved him. He also knew he loved them too.

When she reached him, Shayla threw her arms

around his chest. "Ashy, are you okay?"

He tried to reassure them, but words were hard to come by. "I'm fine. The dove was there…then the large man. Well the next thing I knew, I was outside and Warrior was standing next to me."

Mican interrupted. "Warrior? Is that the really big guy?"

Ashton leaned into the horse and patted his neck. "No, this is Warrior. Isn't he great?"

His brother nodded. "He's great, but where's that really big man? That's who told us you were safe. I wonder where he went?"

Ashton shrugged his shoulders. "Yeah, I know what you mean. One minute he's standing there—the next minute he slips through an invisible screen and *poof,* he's gone."

Mican stepped closer and patted his brother on the back.

Ashton placed his hands on his sister's shoulders and pushed her back so he could see her face. "Shay, I have t'tell you something."

But Mican interrupted again and pointed up.

"Hey guys, look at that."

They instantly turned and witnessed beautiful amber and green leaves falling from nearby trees. The arrow-shaped leaves began to swirl around them in a lovely, gentle spiral of color. As the leaves withdrew, they landed on the ground. The tips of all the leaves pointed in the same direction, forming what appeared to be a path.

A manly voice instructed them. "Follow the trail of leaves."

They glanced around, but didn't see the gigantic man.

Ashton shrugged his shoulders and smiled. "Here we go again." But before he took the lead, he pleaded with Warrior. "Will you come with us?"

The horse bobbed his head.

With his new friend at his side, Ashton led the way. A soft, warm breeze pushed past them. Ashton took a deep breath and let it out through puckered lips. "Man, this is a lot better than the musty smell of the cave."

Shayla and Mican smiled and nodded in

agreement.

Just before another sunset, the never-ending flow of leaves laid down a trail heading into a dense part of a forest. Even in the dim light, the glistening leaves were easy to follow.

Ashton walked along mesmerized. “Man, look at these leaves. They glow from the inside out. I can’t believe how beautiful they are. The colors and the tiny flickers of light are majestic.”

Shayla agreed. “They sparkle, like stardust has fallen to the ground.”

The light from the twinkling leaves pushed away any fear. The scene was breathtaking. The voices of frogs, crickets, and the occasional hoot of an owl, joined the rustle of leaves creating a lovely natural symphony.

With Ashton and Warrior in the lead, they walked out from under the trees. The sun had now fallen below the horizon. It was very dark, except for the sparkle of the tiny specks of light. The trail continued to curve around various bushes and shrubs, but Ashton came to an abrupt stop when they reached the edge of a stream. "Uh-oh, guys."

Leaves landed on the surface of the water, but oddly, they didn't float away. From beside him, Ashton heard the voice again. "Step onto the leaves and cross over. You will be quite safe."

It was Warrior speaking and turned to face him. With arms stretched out at his sides, his voice rose in pitch. "You want us to do what?"

Warrior stepped past him and onto the leaves which remained motionless on top of the water.

Shayla and Mican's mouths dropped open. Mican leaned back and belted out, "Whoa, a leaf-bridge. Go figure."

Ashton's courage rose and he stepped onto the leaves behind Warrior. Shayla and Mican quickly followed. When they reached the other side, they turned and watched the leaves drift away on the current.

With a big grin, Ashton shouted, "That is downright awesome."

Once again, they faced the path and continued to follow Warrior.

When the pleasant path of leaves came to an end, Ashton groaned. "Look guys." There in the distance, the gate awaited them. "At least we don't have to pull vines to get out. The gate doesn't have any on this side," and he laughed.

He and Mican ran forward to open the gate, but stopped in their tracks when it began to swing open without a sound. They glanced over their shoulders.

Warrior had stopped and knelt in front of Shayla. He looked her in the eyes. "It is time to say goodbye, sweet lady."

Her shoulders drooped and her eyes puddled with tears. "Won't you please come with us?"

"I cannot leave the garden, little one."

She stared into Warrior's eyes and tears trickled down her cheeks. "Will we ever see you again?"

"Only if I am sent by the King, but don't be sad. I will always be in your heart. That is where the truth of the Kingdom lives."

Warrior turned to Ashton who now stood close by. "Back in the cave, when you prayed to be saved, the King knew your heart and the full meaning of your request. You are now truly a son of the King. Your name is written in his special Book of Life. Don't let anyone try to tell you that the King and his Kingdom are not real."

Ashton's face lit up in a smile. "I will remember."

The magnificent horse stood, raised his head, and spoke in a firm, but kind tone. "You need to go home now. Your mother will be waiting."

Shayla pushed her arms around Warrior's large chest. Her tears wet his warm hair. "Goodbye, Warrior. I love you." She withdrew her arms from his massive body and ran toward the gate.

Mican took a long, slow look around the garden. He held the gate open for his sister and brother. "It is amazing how much has happened to us here."

Ashton stepped out first and began to squint. Bright daylight greeted him outside the gate. "Wow, how can this be happening?"

His brother and sister joined him and shielded their eyes. The gate closed silently behind them. They watched as the latch clicked shut, and fresh green vines crawled over the wooden barrier. They stared in awe.

A grin filled Ashton's face. "That is so weird, but I love it."

They broke into a run. When they arrived home and approached the kitchen door, they began to yell, "Mom. Mom. We're back." Their feet thumped onto the back porch.

Mom walked into the kitchen as the backdoor swung in. Her hair was tousled, she yawned and stretched. "Well, hey. Where have y'all been?"

They surrounded her with a big group-hug.

Mican launched in, pleading their case. "Mom we are so sorry we were gone so long."

Shayla chimed in. "It was my fault. I'm so sorry."

Ashton added, "But we're all safe. I'm sorry you were worried."

Mom's head drew back, she looked at the clock, but kept her hands on Mican and Ashton's shoulders. Shayla's arms were around her middle. "Whoa. Take it easy. You were gone about twenty minutes, but that's nothing to be so upset about."

"Twenty minutes?" shouted Ashton. "That's impossible. We were gone nearly two days."

"What are you talking about? That's nonsense, silly goose. I would have had the National Guard out looking for you if you had been gone for two days."

She laughed and gave them another group-hug. "Now get washed up. Dinner will be here any minute. It's time," but the ding-dong of the doorbell cut her short. Mom turned to go open the door.

Speechless, they stood in the kitchen, each one knew what had happened, and it couldn't have been only twenty minutes.

Mom yelled from the front door. "Hurry up, you three. I'm hungry."

They turned to go wash up for dinner. Mican and Shayla were still confused, but Ashton's heart overflowed with joy and wonder.

At dinner, Ashton opened his mouth, but Mom interrupted. "Do any of you know who the vandal is that is soaping-up my car windows at night? It's very irritating. Every time I want to go anywhere I have to hose off the car and use a brush to get the side windows clean. I'm getting pretty sick and tired of it. Do you think it might be that kid across the street? What's his name? Key-something?"

Mican said, "Mom, I'm sorry that's happening. I will keep my eyes open to see if I can spot the person who's doing it, but I've never seen Keyon around our driveway or with soap or anything like that."

"Well, maybe not, but I've gone over a couple of times to talk with someone and no one ever comes to the door."

"When I see him, I'll talk to him and let you know what he says."

"Okay, thanks babe. Now, Ash-bug, what were you about to say? I'm sorry I interrupted. I just had to let off a little steam."

"That's okay. Guess what, Mom?"

As she served pizza to his plate, she said, "What, Ash-bug?"

"My name is now written in the King's Book of

Life."

His slice of pizza stopped in midair. "I thought that happened a couple of years ago."

Shayla whipped her head toward him. "I heard Warrior say that. Why did he say it?"

Mom turned her head to face Shayla. "Who's Warrior?"

Ashton took the lead and began to tell their story, with Shayla and Mican adding details. "We saw this dove, y'see, and he led us to this garden."

Shayla added the part about the fish and playing in the stream. Then she told Mom about the mosquito-dents.

Mom leaned toward them and squinted her eyes. "You look fine now."

Ashton paused, but decided to share the part about the dragon, the cave, and the stream. He was afraid the part about the dragon might frighten his mom, but he took a deep breath and told her everything.

Mican and Shayla cheered when Ashton shared the part about ramming the bone up the dragon's nose.

Shayla giggled. "What else happened that we don't know about?"

They were surprised when Ashton told what happened next in the cave. They hadn't seen the dove again, but Ashton said he had. How could they doubt him? After all, they had seen Warrior and the very tall man.

One of Mom's eyebrows arched up, but she didn't say anything.

Then Ashton launched in to his next big revelation. "Shay, I want to thank you for helping to scratch my back and for splashing the water on it."

She tilted her head to the side. "You're welcome, Ashy."

Without warning, Ashton dropped a bombshell. "You have always been good to me, but I've always been jealous of you. I felt like no one ever saw me because Mican is so smart and you are so cute. I'm sorry for how mean I have been to you. Will you forgive me?"

Everyone's mouths fell open, and their eyes

looked like they were staring at a man from outer space.

Ashton asked again, "Will you forgive me, Shay? I love you very much and I'm glad you're my sister."

Shayla shook her head up-and-down a little, as Mom prompted her. "Honey, are you going to answer your brother?"

"Oh. Sure, Ashy, I forgive you and I love you too."

He turned to Mican. "I love you too, bro. I'm sorry for always calling you 'bruh.' I knew you didn't like that, so that's why I did it. And thank you for trying to watch out for me. Will you forgive me for all the times I've, uh, hated you for being so smart and good looking?"

Mican's elbow slipped off of the table and his head bobbed forward, but he managed to regain control. "Sure, dude. I uh, well uh, I love you too, man."

Ashton looked at their mother. "Mom, I love you too, and thank you for being such a great parent."

Her eyes filled with tears and she smiled. "Thank you, Ash-bug. I love you too."

***

Not long after dinner, Mom announced, "Shower time, then off to your rooms."

Happy to be sleeping in their own beds, they gladly complied without arguing.

Through their open bedroom doors, Ashton heard Mom go into Shayla's room across the hall.

Shayla needed no help thinking of something to pray about tonight. She started right in. "Thank you, King, for saving Ashy.

In his room, Ashton smiled.

"Thank you for my mom and thank you for the pile of bones that weren't worthless after all. Oh, and thank you that I don't have to sleep on dry leaves tonight. In the name of your son, amen."

The nightly routine always included a hug. This time when Shayla raised her arms, Mom said, "Shayla, what is that on the back of your arm?"

She reached back to feel. “Yep, that’s a mosquito-dent all right. I must have missed it when I washed in the stream. At least it doesn’t itch anymore. Those things could drive you crazy, they itch so bad.”

“Hmmm, goodnight, sweetheart.” Mom walked to the door and switched off the light.

Across the hall, with prayers finished and the light turned off, they lay quietly in the dark. Finally, Mican broke the silence. “Ash, do you mind talking?”

“No, I don’t mind.” He laughed. “I wondered when you were gonna ask.”

“What happened in the cave that you haven’t told us yet?”

“What makes you think anything else happened?”

“Come on, man. You have been totally different ever since. Now tell me what happened.”

Ashton lowered his voice to a whisper. “I really don’t want Shayla to know this part, okay?

“Okay, Ash. I promise.”

"Well, after I rammed the bone up the dragon's snout, I tried to run, but with my hurt shoulder, I wasn't fast enough. The dragon was able to get the bone out of his nose quicker than I expected. With a powerful blast, he blew it across the cave, it hit me behind my knees and I fell, then his tail slapped me across the floor. That injured my legs and ribs. I ended up with my head dangling over that ledge at the back of the cavern. I couldn't move. There's a deep pit back there, a hot liquid swirls at the bottom, that's where the sulfur smell comes from. I got sick to my stomach from the fumes and threw up. I could hear it hiss when it hit the bottom."

"Sheesh Ash, that's scary."

"Your words came back to me, bro. You said, one day I would get my wish and be alone. There I was, the day I *got my wish*, and it felt like my heart would be crushed from loneliness. I never want to be alone like that again."

"I'm sure that feeling will fade, Ash."

"No, I don't ever want to be that alone again. The only thing that saved me was the dove telling me to call on the King, and you heard the part about the big man being sent to rescue me, but seriously, dude, I didn't think I was gonna make it. A sadness came over me like a heavy blanket. Not sad to be dying, but sad not to be living any more. Does that make sense?"

"I'm not sure."

"It's like when Grammy told us that she knew we would have nice futures. Later she told me that I would grow up to be a very good man. I thought to myself, now all of that future is gone and wasted. I tell you, dying isn't the worst part. Not living is what is sad."

"I get it Ash, and I'm so sorry you went through that."

Ashton surprised Mican. "I'm not, bro. I am a new creature. I tell you my life became clear to me. I never knew how much I was loved, but now I do, and now I know the King. There is no greater gift anyone can have. I'm alive, I have a life, and I'm gonna live. Those are all different things," and his voice trailed off.

Mican reached to turn off the light, then flopped his arm out into the space between their beds. Ashton heard the delivery and knew an outstretched hand waited there. He had never responded to that invitation before, but tonight he flopped his arm to the middle. His fingers smacked Mican's, but more gently than the smack he had given him on the back.

Ashton sniffed and cleared his throat. "Goodnight, Mican."

"Goodnight, Ash."

But Ashton couldn't imagine what would come next.

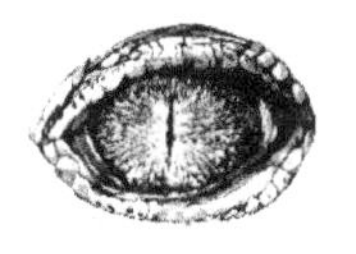

Chapter 9

Ashton's Dream

Ashton jolted awake, his eyes flew open and he sat up in bed. A dream lingered in his mind, so vivid it included the sweet fragrance of red roses, purple iris, and white tulips, mingled with the tangy, richness of the thick, green grass. He could hardly wait to tell Mican and Shayla.

He crept across the hall into Shayla's room. His toes burrowed into the thick, pink carpet, cushioning his bare feet and muffling any sound. When he reached the side of her bed, he tugged on the corner of her pillow and leaned over. "Shay, wake up. I need to talk to you."

Shayla barely moved. "Ashyyyyy, nooo. Go away."

"I can't. I have too much to tell you. Come to our room and hurry."

She groaned with her eyes still closed. "Whyyyy? I'm sleepy."

"Warrior spoke to me. I have to tell you what he said."

He turned and ran to the door, but tiptoed back across the hall. There he tugged on Mican's pillow. Mican gave a backward swat, which Ashton dodged. The blow missed its intended target. "Stop, Ash. Leave me alone."

Shayla stumbled into the boys' room and plopped facedown across Ashton's bed. Her curls bounced, but landed hanging off the bed. "What is it? Why did you wake me up?"

"I had a dream. I have to tell you about it."

Mican mumbled in a voice laced with a groan. "It wasn't a dream, Ash. We were all there."

"Noooooo!" Ashton shook Mican's bed with force. "Warrior spoke to me in a dream. He wants us to come back to the garden. He said the King wants to see us."

Mican startled awake. “What? Are you nuts?”

Ashton waved his hands in front of Mican. “Shhhhhh. Don’t wake up Mom.”

Wide awake now, Shayla whispered loudly. “Are you crazy? Yesterday I was afraid I had gotten you killed and you want us to go back to that place?”

“No, not me. It’s Warrior. He said for us to come back. He said the King wants to talk with us.”

As he looked at his brother, Mican’s eyes narrow. “The King wants to talk to us, or to you?”

Ashton remained adamant. “Warrior told me the King wants to see all three of us.”

With a blank expression, Mican rolled onto his side. “So how do we do this? What do we tell Mom?” No one answered, so he continued. “Maybe we should slip out and leave a note. What do you think, Ash?”

He shook his head. “No way. We don’t want to start our trip to see the King with a lie. Nope, no way. We do this right, or we don’t do it at all. We have to tell Mom the truth.”

Shayla added, “And get her permission, right Ashy?”

Ashton bobbed his head once. “Right.”

While discussing how they should tell, or ask, their mom about going to the garden, they heard her voice. “Hey, my little ducklings, are you awake?”

Their voices answered together. “Yes, Ma’am.”

“Get ready for breakfast. I’m fixing something special. We are celebrating this morning.”

Shayla dashed to her room to dress and the boys scrambled to get ready, before heading to the kitchen.

Mican, being the oldest and the fastest, pushed Ashton back with a playful grin and arrived first.

“What’s for breakfast? What are we celebrating?”

“Good morning to you too.”

He dipped his chin to his chest and his eyes glanced at the floor. “Sorry Mom. Good morning. What’s for breakfast?”

“We definitely need to work on your manners, Mr. Mican-bee.”

His brother laughed, as he slid into his usual chair. “That’s not all that needs work.”

“And for you Mr. Ash-bug, we need to,” but Shayla’s cheerful voice interrupted her.

“Morning, Momma.”

Mom looked lovingly at all three of her babes, as she called them. Although they were far from being babies now. Even Shayla had grown into a lovely, ten-year-old, young lady.

“Good morning, my three ba….”

Ashton interrupted with a sigh. “Pleeease don’t say, ‘babes,’ Mom. It’s embarrassing.”

“Okay, my three—blessings. How’s that? Good morning. We are having French Toast this morning to celebrate Ashton’s name being in the King’s special book.”

They smiled at the mention of French Toast, then glanced at each other. They knew the King wanted to see them, but they still didn’t know how to bring it up.

Ashton sat waiting for the tasty treat, but began to get uneasy about their trip to the garden. “Mom I need to ask you something."

Mom served herself last, then sat down. "What's up Ash-bug, and what are your plans for this fine Saturday?"

Mican and Shayla stared at their plates, but that gave Ashton the perfect opening he'd been waiting for.

He looked her straight in the eyes. "Mom, I had a dream. The King sent Warrior to tell me he wanted to see us. We need to go back to the garden." Glancing at his siblings, then back to their Mom, he asked, "Would that be okay?"

She smiled. "Well, if the King wants to see you, by all means you must go. Don't you three agree?"

They nodded and a broad smile crossed Ashton's face. "Thanks Mom. You're the best."

They finished eating breakfast and Mican asked, "Mom, can we be excused?"

"That's *may* we be excused? And yes, you may."

Terrible scraping sounds erupted, as they

pushed their chairs away from the table.

Mom frowned. “Hey, easy, pleasey.”

Each apologized and gently slipped their chair into place, then gave Mom a morning hug.

After they finished brushing their teeth, Ashton yelled, “Let’s go, slow pokes.”

Shayla swung into her room and grabbed a sweater.

They headed through the kitchen where Mom still sipped her coffee and reached for the door, but Mom stopped them. “Whoa, you three. A little help here.”

When they finished putting their dishes in the dishwasher, they pushed the screen door open and dashed into the backyard. The door slammed shut with a loud *bang*.

Yells followed. “Bye, Momma. We love you.”

Mican had assured them that he could find his way back to the garden.

As they jogged into the woods, Shayla talked to her brothers. “I’m glad we didn’t lie to Momma, or try to sneak off. That makes me feel better about going back to the garden. I think when I pushed past you Mican and rushed into the garden, I placed us all in danger, especially you, Ashy. I've learned a very important lesson. I'm going to be more careful."

Ashton nodded. "Good deal, Shay. Now stop talking and let's get there."

They trotted side-by-side for a few minutes, until Shayla decided to make it a race.

"Hey come back here," yelled Mican. "You can't go in without us."

She froze in her tracks.

When her brothers jogged past her, Ashton said, "Come on, Shay. Stay with us."

She dashed to catch up.

A few seconds later, Mican stopped. "Guys, this trail doesn't look right." He glanced around.

Ashton turned to his brother. "Which way do you think we should go?"

The crack of a branch alerted Mican to a presence, he turned, and a wolf approached. He called to his brother. "Ash, get Shay out of here," as he picked up a large stick to defend himself."

"No can do, bro. I'm a little busy."

A wolf of equal size crept slowly in, ready to pounce on Ashton.

Shayla cleared her throat. "Mican, how are we going to get to the King?"

He glanced over his shoulder and backed toward her. "Shay, come with me."

Suddenly the wolf, now in front of him, crouched to pounce.

Without warning, the dove appeared, he flared his wings and swooped between Mican and the wolf. "Back away, Magnus Wolf." He turned his gaze in Ashton's direction. "Back away Morgan, brother of Magnus, or this will not end well for you. Return to your den."

The wolves slunk back, then turned and ran.

Mican breathed a sigh of relief. "Whew, we're glad to see you."

"You three seem to have taken a wrong turn." He joyfully pointed out the right direction. "Come this way please."

Ashton smiled and said, "With pleasure," and they broke into a run, but this time following behind the dove.

After a few minutes, Mican and Ashton reached the gate.

Shayla hurried to stand at their side. Her chest rose and fell heavily, but she tried to hide it.

The gate, again covered with vines required work, but this time the fresh, green growth broke away easier.

Ashton smiled as he pulled. "This smell reminds me of fresh cut grass."

Shayla wrinkled her eyebrows. "Are you sure we are supposed to go in, Ashy? Maybe those wolves were a sign. And where did the dove go?"

His arms tightened as he pulled a vine and answered her. "Warrior said for us to come. The King wants to see us."

Mican paused from the work, his shoulders, tightly drawn toward his ears betrayed his stress and he asked, "Are you sure it wasn't *just* a dream?"

That did it. Ashton snapped at him. "As sure as I

can be until we try."

"I have an idea," said Mican. "Why don't you call Warrior and see if he answers from behind the wall?"

"I have to admit, that sounds like a good plan, bro." He cupped his hands to his mouth and shouted, "Warrior. Are you there? This is Ashton. Are you waiting for us?" But no answer came.

Shayla encouraged him. "Try again, Ashy, a little louder this time."

He cupped his hands around his mouth and tipped his head back. "War-rior, can you hear me?" But again, no answer came.

Adding her own touch, Shayla shouted, "Waaar-riorrr." Still no reply.

"Ash, if Warrior told you the King wants to see us, shouldn't he be waiting for us?"

His face tightened; his voice came out rude and abrupt. "I don't know, Mican. Maybe we have to go inside the garden before he can hear me."

Shayla risked sharing her concern. "I don't know either, Ashy. I think we should go home."

Their lack of belief caused him to shout. “But Warrior said for us to come.” He jerked the final vine from the gate. Anticipating a struggle, Ashton reached forward and grabbed the latch, but it lifted easily.

They stood there, wide-eyed and speechless as the gate glided into the garden.

Mican finally broke the silence with a laugh. “It looks like the gate was expecting us, but do you want me to go first, Ash?”

He nodded and Mican stepped into the garden.

“What do you see, bro?”

His brother glanced around. “The same as yesterday, but without the dragon.”

Ashton’s eyes narrowed and he placed his hand over his mouth and chin. “Maybe the big man with the sword killed the dragon.”

Being comforted by that thought, Ashton and Shayla stepped in behind Mican. Ashton looked all around, then decided. “We can’t just stand here.”

“I agree we can’t but,” Mican glanced at him. “I thought Warrior would be here. What do you think we should do?"

He stepped past Mican. "I think we should go this way." He pointed straight ahead.

Following his lead, Mican and Shayla stayed close behind and watched for any sign of trouble.

Before they reached another bend in the trail, Mican attempted to make a joke. "Maybe we should have brought some breadcrumbs to follow on our way back."

His brother laughed. "Knowing our luck, birds would eat them." Then from out of nowhere, a swarm of savage gnats descended on them and attacked. Ashton shouted, "Their bites feel like little pin-sticks all over."

Shayla swatted and yelled. "Stop it, you crazy gnats. Stop it."

Mican grabbed her by the arm. "Run."

Head first, Ashton took the lead. "This way. Come through here." They jumped from the path and crashed through bushes. "Man, these briars grab at my pants legs and the higher limbs pull my hair."

They got scratched and whacked by branches, as

they rushed through the bushes to fight off the biting bugs. After running for a few yards, Ashton pushed aside a large branch and there stood a most welcomed sight. Warrior waited for them in a grassy clearing.

When Mican and Shayla caught up, they noticed they had also lost the gnats.

Ashton ran forward and threw his arms around the horse's neck. "Warrior, we called you, but you didn't answer."

Warrior lowered his head close to Ashton's face. The breath from the horse's nostrils smelled like fresh cut hay and had a strange comforting effect. Ashton relaxed against the warm soft mane.

"I could not, my boy. I cannot answer calls like that from beyond the wall. By faith you must enter into this world. Did I not speak to you in your dream and tell you the King wanted you to come?"

Ashton lowered his eyes. "Yes, you told me."

"Then you must trust what's in your spirit and respond." Warrior gave him a loving nudge with his nose.

With warm cheeks and rounded shoulders, Ashton answered. "I was trying, but we were a little scared."

"That is understandable. You're still very young, yet you overcame your fear and entered the garden. That was a leap of faith. Each step you took to find me was a step of faith. Very good, young man. Very well done."

Not expecting this kind of praise, Ashton smiled and grabbed Warrior around the neck, giving him another big hug.

"Thank you for the hugs. Now we must go." Warrior knelt beside Shayla. "Climb onto my back, little one." She crawled onto his back and sat up straight. Warrior got to his hooves. "Mican, Ashton, you walk beside me, this way, lads."

Shayla began to scratch. "Boys, I forgot to tell you Momma found another mosquito-dent on the back of my arm last night. I don't know if it is my imagination, but the bite is starting to itch again. I think it is because of those darn gnats."

Ashton wrinkled his nose and rubbed his right

shoulder. "I know what you mean, my shoulder hurts more now than it did last night. It has to be this place."

As they walked through the woods, Mican questioned Warrior. "What was up with the wolves? We didn't see them yesterday. And those gnats? They bite something fierce for little guys. They tried to eat us alive today."

Warrior cast a glance back over his shoulder. "Each day has its own problems. Like yesterday you encountered the dragon who is in the garden."

Shayla's eyes popped open wide and her shoulders jumped. "What do you mean, 'the dragon who *IS* in the garden?' You mean he's not dead?"

"Oh no, he is very much alive."

Ashton shook his head. "I can't believe that big man didn't kill him."

Warrior's calm reassuring voice explained. "I understand your concerns, but no, the Guardian did not kill him. The King simply sent him to rescue you from the dragon."

Dread filled Ashton's voice. "Are we gonna run

into him again?"

Warrior stopped to answer. He turned to look straight into Ashton's eyes. "You need to learn how to avoid the evil dragon and not give him any inroad into your life. If you let him, the dragon will gain a foothold from which he can lead you."

Ashton tilted his head and his eyebrows drew closer together. "What type of inroad? What do you mean by foothold?"

Warrior tried to make it clear. "Any time you are disobedient, or if you are mean to someone, or if you tell a lie, you are giving evil an inroad. That gives the dragon a way to interfere in your life. Do you understand?"

Ashton's forehead wrinkled. "I think so."

Warrior turned back to the path and continued to walk. "Now as I was saying about the wolves and the gnats. Each day has its own problems. Some will be major like the wolves, some will be minor like the gnats, and some will be painful, but you must learn how to handle each one as the King gives you direction."

Ashton's mouth pulled slightly to one side. "Why did the King call for us?"

Warrior answered. "It is time to begin your training."

Mican's attention was stirred. "What training?"

Not willing to answer for the King, Warrior simply said, "Patience. You will see."

Shayla grinned. "So, our training will in 'patience'?" and she giggled.

Warrior looked over his shoulder. One eye stared at Shayla. It caused her face to turn pink.

"As I said, you will see."

Mican and Ashton walked silently beside Warrior. All the while, they scanned the area trying to find landmarks or signs to follow on their way back.

Without even looking back, Warrior seemed to know. "No need to search for signs or markers to follow, lads. And you certainly didn't need to bring breadcrumbs."

Mican stared at his feet. "Oh, you heard that?"

"Certainly. I have been sent by the King to

watch over you and guide you, once you entered into the garden by faith."

Ashton scratched his chin and tried to be sure he understood. "So, are you saying that it is your job to take us to the King?"

Warrior answered. "Not exactly. It is my job to be sure that your faith takes you to the King."

"I'm not sure I understand."

"It is quite simple, Ashton. It took faith to accept the King's dream. It also took faith to ask your mom's permission to come to the garden today. By the way, that was the right thing to do. Once you took your first step toward the garden, you were also walking in faith."

Ashton's chin dipped toward his chest. "Did I show a lack of faith when I stood outside the garden and called for you?"

If a horse could smile, Warrior did. "A little bit, but after all you are young and you need to grow in faith. Still you overcame your fear and reached for the gate latch. That was a very bold step of faith, Ashton, especially with Mican and Shayla doubting you. That was very bold indeed."

Mican and Shayla turned their eyes toward the ground. Shayla said, "Sorry, Ashy."

Mican agreed. "Me too, dude."

Shayla lifted her face and all of a sudden, she saw from Warrior's back what the boys could not yet see.

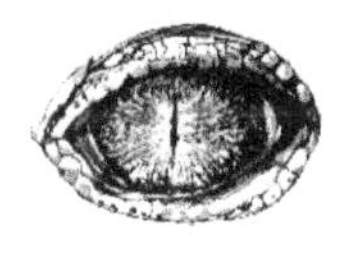

Chapter 10

Time for Training

Shayla placed her hands on her cheeks and exclaimed, “Oh my, it’s so beautiful.”

“What is it? What do you see?” The boys rushed forward and climbed onto a boulder next to the path. They now saw the breathtaking scene stretched out at the bottom of the hill.

Ashton shouted, “Look at that lake. It is crystal clear, and it sparkles like diamonds are floating on top.” The water reflected the brilliance of sunlight.

A fresh, cool breeze rose up the hill and washed over them. The rush of air carried a sweet and inviting perfumed scent.

“That smells amazing.” Shayla murmured. "And it tastes like cinnamon sugar, like Momma puts on toast. Boys, can you taste it?"

Ashton opened his mouth. "That's amazing! I *can* taste it, Shay. Awesome, but where does all that sunlight come from? Look how it reflects off the water. It seems to be all around, everywhere at the same time, but I can't see the sun. Can you guys see it?"

Mican cocked his head and pointed. "The sun must be behind that fortress, Ash. See how it glows behind there? But, man! Look at that river. Where does that come from?"

At the far end of the lake on the opposite shore, a river flowed through a trench, down the smooth green hillside and into the water. Their eyes skimmed the high hill to find the source.

Shayla lifted her arm and pointed. "Hey boys, the river looks like it runs out from under the huge wall of that fort up there."

"Awesome," shouted Ashton.

"Boys, be gentlemen. Help your sister down."

Shayla swung her left leg across Warrior's neck. Mican stuck both arms up and prepared to catch her.

"Lean forward Shay and put your hands on my shoulders as you slide off."

Ashton stood close by in case she needed help, but Shayla slipped off without a problem. Mican placed his hands at her waist and her feet landed softly on the ground.

"Now children, walk down that path, to the water's edge and you will be helped across."

Ashton's shoulders drop as he glanced at Warrior. "But aren't you coming with us? I thought you were supposed to watch over us and guide us to the King."

Warrior leveled his eyes lovingly at him. "And that is exactly what I am doing, now down the hill to the lake. Take your next step of faith." He turned before they could argue any further and walked into the woods.

Without delay, they set off. It took a few minutes to descend the curvy, but well-trodden path. When they arrived at the lake, they searched for a way across.

Ashton turned to face back up the hill and

shouted. "Warrior, what now? How do we get across?"

From one side, he heard a sweet, high pitched voice. "Warrior is not here, but will I do?"

Ashton quickly turned around and joined his brother and sister.

They looked in the direction of the new voice and saw a very, large swan swimming toward them.

Ashton's eyebrows seemed to rise with the pitch of his voice. "Uhhh, hello."

The swan coasted to a stop at the water's edge. "Hello. My name is Ozwan. I've been expecting you."

"So, you are Ozwan—the swan?"

"Yes, I am, and you must be Ashton. The King has sent me to fetch the three of you."

"So, you are the dog, and we are the sticks that you were sent to fetch. That's funny."

Ozwan dipped her beak and glared at him. "Yes, this one is definitely Ashton."

He jabbed his open hands out to the side. "Hey, what does that mean?"

Mican and Shayla glanced at each other and laughed.

Ashton wrinkled his forehead and flashed a look at them. "Okay, watch it, you two."

Mican addressed the swan. "How can you carry all three of us?"

"I can't. But …." Ozwan gave a long, loud honk and two, enormous geese flew into view. They landed on the lake and coasted to a stop next to her.

"Shayla dear, will you climb onto my back, and boys, will you choose your rides please?"

Ozwan extended her wing to the shore, but Shayla took a step back and shook her head *no.* "I don't want to hurt you."

The swan tipped her head to the side. "How sweet you are. You will not hurt me, my dear. Don't be afraid. Now come quickly."

The two geese did the same for the boys, then off they glided in a silent motion.

In front of them, Shayla had the appearance of a princess on her throne as she sat perched between Ozwan's massive wings.

After rubbing her hand along the length of a white velvety feather, Shayla accidentally stroked its edge when she drew her hand back. The edge of the feather felt like the edge of a paper fan, strangely rough, but not sharp. Ozwan showed no sign of it hurting or being offensive in any way.

While studying the water, Ashton noticed that it had small waves that trailed behind each bird as it swam. Otherwise, the lake appeared smooth as glass and the water, so clear he could see the bottom. But stranger still, he became aware that if he adjusted his eyes, he could see his own reflection on the surface. It depended on how deep he looked into the water. "Hey guys, look at the water. You can see your reflection."

Mican did and said, "So?"

"Now, look past your face and deeper into the water. You can see the bottom."

Mican gave it a try. "That's cool."

"Yeah, isn't it?"

Shayla ignored their conversation and scanned the scenery all around her. "This is the most beautiful place on earth."

Without turning her head, Ozwan said, "So, you assume you are on earth?"

"Well, I guess so," replied Shayla. As they coasted to a graceful stop at the opposite shore, she asked, "If we are not on earth, where are we?"

Ozwan extended her wing to the bank and Shayla stepped off. "You shall be told in time."

Then the geese arrived, and the boys stepped ashore.

Ashton asked, "What now?"

Ozwan spoke as she paddled away from the shoreline. "Look behind you, young man."

They looked and noticed a cloud coming toward them. Ashton turned the corners of his mouth down. "What now? Rain?"

When the cloud got closer, they could tell it consisted of small, individual creatures.

Shayla shouted. "It's a herd of butterflies."

Ashton couldn't resist teasing. "Of course, I've heard of butterflies."

Mican laughed. "Very funny, Ash."

Shayla parked her fists on her hips. "Okay, what would you call a herd of butterflies, Mr. Smarty Pants?" But suddenly with a gasp, she corrected herself. "Ashy, I'm sorry. That was funny."

Ashton's shoulders jerked back straightening his body and he stared at her. "What? Is that all you're gonna say?"

Shayla's reply wiped the smile from his face. "I don't want to give the evil dragon a foothold."

That struck him in the heart. "Oh, okay, I get it."

Mican said, "At the risk of being called a Mr. Smarty Pants, a group of butterflies is called a kaleidoscope." Then he chuckled.

In the very next moment, beautiful butterflies surrounded them, each appeared unique.

The most marvelous butterfly they had ever seen flew directly toward Ashton. At least fifteen inches tall, the wings wafted the air as it floated in front of him and introduced itself. "My name is Patrice. The King has sent me to guide you to the palace. We will follow the narrow path. Please come this way."

Ashton bowed with one arm across his waist, as he rose, he swished his other hand toward the top of the mountain. "Lead onward."

Shayla giggled and Mican groaned.

He scowled and twisted his lips. "Knock it off, you two."

A long and winding, pebble-covered path led up the mountain.

In the distance ahead, a stone fortress stood tall, with beauty and majesty.

Occasionally, a butterfly's soft wing brushed their cheek or one darted in front of their eyes, and the sunlight took on the color of its thin, silken wings.

As they topped the hill, the butterfly cloud lifted. They now saw that the wall which they had seen in the distance, surrounded a grand castle.

Ashton faced Patrice. "How do we get there from here?"

The lovely butterfly floated in front of him and spoke with a tiny, gentle voice. "Follow the dragonfly on this path to the gate. A friend will meet you there."

Immediately a dragonfly with a light green body and sheer golden wings, glided to a stop in front of them. With the strength and boldness of a Viking, it announced, "My name is Omuth. Would you please follow me?"

Walking only a few feet behind him, they made their way down the narrow walkway to the castle wall. It only took a few minutes to reach the gate, when they arrived Omuth paused and faced them. "Here you are, children. Are you ready for your next step of faith?"

Remembering what Warrior had said, Ashton reached for the latch, but before he touched it, the gate slowly began to creak open. Shayla held her breath, unnecessarily.

There in the courtyard, beyond the gate, stood their friend. Ashton ran to him and threw his arms around the horse's warm neck. "How did you get here before us?"

Shayla dashed to Warrior's side. "Why couldn't we have come all the way with you?"

"Do you remember what I told you about faith? It took a growth in faith to get you here. Staying with me would not have been faith; it would have been familiar and comfortable." Warrior gave a soft whinny, then shook his head and mane. "The King is most pleased with you."

Ashton leaned back so he could see Warrior's eyes. "I get it. I had to trust in the dream and in each of the creatures the King sent to guide us here."

"Come now, you need to get into the castle. The King is expecting you."

The corners of Ashton's mouth sloped down. "Aren't you coming in with us?"

Warrior lowered his head to Ashton's face. "No, lad, you and your brother and sister will go alone from here."

Shayla twisted her hands together and stared at the ground. "Warrior, what is the King like? Is he mean?"

"No, precious one. Only when someone tries to hurt little ones, like you, does the King get really angry." Warrior nuzzled Shayla and she gave him a kiss on the nose, then he gave her a nudge. "Go now. The King is waiting."

They slowly walked toward the door of the castle. As they climbed the large stone steps, the heavy wooden door swung inward. Shayla grabbed Mican's hand, then stretched her other hand back toward Ashton. He willingly took hold.

With a quick glance back at Warrior, they crossed through the massive opening into the castle entryway.

A long, scarlet-red rug led the way to narrow double doors that reached toward the ceiling. With a slow, smooth movement, they opened. Stepping inside, the sight amazed them. They realized they stood in the throne room of the King.

The brightness and noisiness dazzled their senses. In fact, the brightness caused them to partially close their eyes, but only for a few seconds. Once their eyes adjusted to the brightness, they could see that the room gleamed with white, satiny marble floors and walls. Columns of white alabaster dotted the room.

Ashton poked his brother and shouted. "Dude, look. There are pictures of angels, carved into these posts, but they are not women. These are men angels, strong and brave-looking."

Mican stared for a moment, then leaned toward his brother. "Look at the gold around the bottoms of all the pillars. The color radiates with a glow into the room. It glistens from every inch of molding around the floor and around every column."

His brother leaned back and pointed. "And gold completely covers the domed ceiling. It is brighter in here than the clearest sunny day."

Another amazing sight grabbed Mican's attention. He pointed toward two chairs. "Look! There's a river flowing from under those crystal thrones."

As it bubbled up, it caused a light mist to rise above the royal seats, forming a halo or cloud above the majestic thrones.

Mican's gaze followed the water. "The water has cut a path in the marble, or one has been cut for it, it's hard to tell which. Look how it flows without a sound, like a clear, liquid ribbon crossing the floor."

The water ran toward the far end of the room. There, it disappeared under the wall or through it. Again, they could not tell.

Because of the noisiness of the throne room, Mican shouted, "This must be the source of the river that flowed down the mountain and into the lake."

Too shocked to say anything for a moment, Shayla's attention wandered to a large group of men. They stood before the two seated on the thrones. She counted, "One, two, three …."

Twenty-four older people gathered before the King and the Prince. They sang and shouted praises to the two men seated on the thrones. Their songs and shouts of joy filled the room, as the fresh scent of flowers floated through the air.

Ashton stood in one spot, but turned around to admire every inch of the throne room. "Amazing! Simply amazing." Then he locked eyes with one of the men. "He must be the King," yelled Ashton.

Mican shouted, “The one to his right must be his Son. I wonder why the King called us here?”

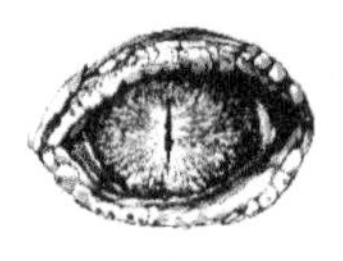

Chapter 11

Meeting the King

The King leaned forward on his throne and spoke to the older people gathered before him. Without any argument, they began to leave the room. When the doors closed behind them, the King waved his hand and beckoned them. In a strong, but kind voice he announced. “Come closer, children. My Son tells me good things about you.”

He watched as they walked the long distance from the double doors to the thrones. They stopped and stood before him.

“My boy, you received my dream and came to me as I asked. I am greatly pleased.”

Ashton stared at the King in surprise, but he politely responded. “Thank you, Sir.”

He addressed both Mican and Ashton. “You two boys, are fine lads, but young and untrained.”

At that moment, the King’s attention turned to Shayla standing next to her brothers, but staring at the floor.

“My dear child, you appear as though you are worried. Do you have a question?”

Shayla gripped her hands in front of her and looked up. “I do, Sir.”

“What is it, little one? What is worrying you?”

“Ozwan corrected me at the lake when I said this was ‘the most beautiful place on earth.’ So, I was wondering, if we’re not on earth anymore, Sir, have we died and gone to heaven?

He leaned back in his seat and smiled. “No, child.”

“Where are we then? If you don’t mind me asking.”

“This is my Kingdom, dear girl. This realm is part of heaven, but not where those who have died go to live forever. This is my throne room, my dwelling place. It is a part of my kingdom, and it is more real than anything you have ever known before. You need to learn that you are merely a sojourner or traveler, passing through, on earth. This is now your true home."

Her face tightened again, and her eyes looked like a scared rabbit. "If this is our home now, will we ever be able to go back to see our mother again?"

The King's smile became even wider. "Yes, certainly, my child. This is a place where you may come by faith, to seek help and wisdom. It is a spiritual kingdom or realm that can only be reached after a person has been called by my Spirit and has then received my Son into his or her heart."

They all nodded to show they understood, but Shayla said, "Thank you for your answer, Sir."

The King now addressed all three. "Your mother, and your father before he came to live with me, have done well with you, many children do not have the same type of family you three have had. For them, it is sometimes more difficult to find me. I have a mission for you, I want you to help bring others to me, but you still have much to learn and now it is time to begin your training. Ashton was the last of you to call upon my Son. Remember when you and Ashton first called upon my Son? I knew that Ashton did not yet truly believe in his heart, so I did not receive him. All he did that day was to join the group."

Shayla said, "Really?"

"At that time, I *was* calling you, Shayla. When you called upon my Son, I heard you, and I knew that in your heart, you believed and understood. It was then that I received you, but if you had not believed in your heart, I would not have received you either."

Shayla lifted her head and locked eyes with the King. "Yes Sir. Thank you."

"I have a saying that describes what Ashton has now experienced. 'He who is forgiven much, loves much.' Ashton had a dramatic awakening. He also knew that he had been forgiven of many things."

Mican looked up at the King and asked, "What about me, Sir?"

"Yes, Mican, you were the first to believe in my Son. Your heart was tender and pure. Even at five years of age, you understood a great deal more than some lads twice your age. You are a true treasure, my boy."

Mican looked down and his face flashed pink. "Thank you, Sir."

Ashton asked, "Sir, I thank you for saving me, but can I ask you a question?"

"Certainly, my boy. What is it?"

"Why did our dad die?"

Mican and Shayla's heads snapped toward him.

"Well thank you for asking me, rather than blaming me, son. It was not my wish that your father be killed in that accident, but people have a free will. I also don't want to blame your father, but at that time, he did not listen to me when I told him not to go to the meeting on that snowy night. People get so caught up in worldly things, they forget to listen to me about what I would like for them to do. There is more that you will learn later about his accident, but for now, know that I treasured your father."

Mican's eyes filled with tears. "I remember, Mom wanted him to stay home. They didn't know I was listening, but I heard him say he was worried about *what might happen* if he didn't go."

"Yes, that is what he told her. I would have preferred that he stayed home. I would have taken care of what he worried about, but I can tell you now, he is most proud of the three of you for how you have carried on without him. And Ashton, he wants you to grieve less for him. That is why he wanted you to know how much you are loved. You no longer need to think of him and your Grammy as your only friends."

"Yes Sir, I see, but I still miss him very much. Can I ask why you didn't protect him? You knew what was gonna happen, right?"

"Oh, my dear boy. There are different reasons for different deaths, but with your dad, it hurt so badly to watch. When someone walks outside of my will, I have no control over their lives, until they submit to me again. It was at that brief moment, when your dad was not under my leadership, that he had his accident. The evil one seized the opportunity to take his life, but in the midst of his accident, he asked me to forgive him for not being obedient, so he did come to live with me. As time goes by, it will hurt less, but you will always love him, my boy. He also knows that."

Ashton stared at the floor. "Thank you, Sir. I'm glad to know that he is watching over me. Does he have wings?"

"My boy, I did not say that he is watching over you, that is my job, but he was aware that you were in pain, and he wanted you to know that you are not alone and that you are loved. As for the wings, that would be a 'no.' He is not an angel. Angels are created beings. When people die, those who believe in and follow me and my Son, come to live in a special place here, but angels are not your dead friends and relatives. Don't be deceived, thinking a dead person is your guardian angel. That is not true. Angels are beings that I created for special purposes. Now does that answer your questions?"

"Yes, Sir. Thank you."

The King turned his attention again toward Shayla. "You, Shayla, were the first to ask me to rescue Ashton."

This is the first time Ashton had heard this, and he turned to look at her with his mouth open.

"You have a truly noble heart, young lady. In time, you will be a good example for young women everywhere. You also asked for forgiveness for getting Ashton into trouble, which you have been granted. Know that you are forgiven and don't allow the evil one to torture your spirit.

"Remember when Ashton teased you about the 'herd of butterflies,' you snapped at him. You also quickly asked him to forgive you. You have learned much already, and as you grow, you will have much wisdom you can share with others."

"Thank you."

"Shayla, my dear," the King paused and stared at her.

"Yes, Sir?"

He motioned for her to step forward. "Before

you go, I need to take care of something for you. Come here and lift your sleeve."

The boys now saw the dent on the back of her arm.

The King leaned to his side and dipped his fingers into the river that flowed from under his throne. He touched his fingertips to the dent, then the King caught a thorn that popped out.

He held it up and showed it to them. "This is a fiery dart of the enemy." He grinned at Shayla. "I could not leave it in one so precious to me."

Shayla lit up, a smile swept across her face. "Thank you very much, Sir."

"Be sure to show your mother your arm. She needs to see it."

Then the King turned to Ashton. "Now for you, my boy, step forward." The King dipped his fingers again into the water. "Will you push your shirt collar aside, please?"

He did and the King touched his shoulder with the water.

Ashton's eyes brightened, he lifted his arm and

moved it around. "Wow. That feels great. Thank you!"

The King smiled. "Now, it is time for you to leave. You have only been gone for a few minutes in your time, but your mom will be waiting."

Mican tipped his head to the side. "Why is the time different here? Is there no time here?"

"Quite the opposite, my boy, I am the creator of time. I know the beginning and the end; I see all of time. Now it is *time* for you to go."

Ashton laughed. "I get it. That's funny."

Shayla got excited. "Will Warrior take us home?"

"No, dear one, my Spirit will guide you."

The dove who led them to the garden the first time, appeared, fluttered down, and settled on the King's shoulder.

Mican's muscles tightened. "Sir, are you sure we are to follow him? He left us in the garden the first time and that got us into trouble."

The King propped his elbows on the arms of his throne and leaned forward, but spoke gently to him.

"If you will remember, Mican, my Spirit did not leave you in the garden. You three left him to follow the fish and to play in the stream. He tried to get you to follow him, but you did not. At that time, you failed to realize the importance of following my Spirit."

He knew the truth of what the King said and hung his head. Mican finally looked up. "Yes, Sir. That is true. We are very sorry. Please forgive us."

The King leaned back and smiled. "You are forgiven!" And as he lifted his arm, the dove rose into the air and flew toward the door. The boys turned to follow him.

The King waved and said, "Remember to follow my Spirit."

Before she turned, Shayla paused and addressed the King. "Sir, what should we call you? Shall we call you King, or Your Majesty? Or what?"

The boys paused to listen.

The King's eyes crinkled at the corners as he smiled. "All three of you may call me Abba."

She cocked her head. "Abba. What does that

mean?"

"It is 'Abba Father,' a term that I love. It is like when you were younger, you crawled up into your father's lap and called him, Daddy."

Shayla smiled, "Yes Sir, I mean, yes Abba." She quickly joined her brothers, and they followed the dove out of the castle. He led them through the gate and down the hill, to a bridge. Beneath the bridge flowed the crystal, clear river.

Ashton took in a deep breath. "Wow, the mist from the river smells great."

They stopped for a moment on the bridge and gazed at the silent, beautiful sight.

The dove led on, and when they reached the bottom of the hill, their path wound alongside the lake. Shayla opened her mouth to make a remark, but paused, then stated, "This is the most beautiful realm that I've ever seen." She glanced at the dove. "Would that be the correct way to say it?"

"Yes, dear girl, that will do. You may refer to this place as a realm, or a kingdom. Either or both is correct. And it *is* indeed beautiful."

As they continued to follow the dove, their path began to curve away from the lake, up a hill, and into a forest. Ashton glanced back at the sparkling water. "Is the path Warrior used when he left us to meet Ozwan on the other side of the lake?"

Neither of his siblings answered and the dove didn't volunteer.

The next stretch of path took them through a peaceful forest. "Oooo, boys, this smells amazing, almost like peppermint."

After what seemed like only a few minutes, they re-entered the garden. Much to their displeasure, they found the gnats waiting.

Mican yelled, "Run."

He and Shayla took off, but Ashton watched as the dove ate the gnats one-by-one.

When Mican and Shayla noticed Ashton standing still, they stopped. They watched, as the dove gobbled up the last two gnats.

Ashton looked at Mican and laughed. "I wish we had known about the dove when we came through here before."

Mican laughed too. “I know what you mean. We can add that to the list of things we have already learned.”

About that time Shayla spotted the garden gate and dashed toward it.

This prompted the dove. “Careful, little one.”

She turned and pointed. “But the gate is right there.”

Remember what the King said, “Never get ahead of the Spirit, wait for me, there is a zeal that runs ahead of Abba,[i] don’t assume you know what to do.”

Shayla nodded. “I’m sorry, Spirit.”

When her brothers caught up with her, the Spirit beamed with pride. “Very good, little one. You may go now. Your mother is waiting.”

Shayla reached for the gate latch, but withdrew her hand. She turned to the dove with a twinkle in her eyes. “Spirit, will you please open the gate?”

The dove flitted to the latch. “It will be my great pleasure, dear one.”

The dove fluttered in, touched it lightly with his

wing, and it obeyed by swinging into the garden.

Mican, Ashton, and Shayla stepped through the gate. They stood for a moment, watching with wide-eyes. As the gate closed, vines twisted their way across the wood and covered it once again.

"That is so weird," whispered Ashton. Then he grinned and added, "But I love it."

Back on the world's side of the gate, they shivered from the cold. Since they didn't know exactly how long they'd been gone, Mican motioned for Shayla and Ashton to run with him toward home.

When they reached the backyard, they ran toward the steps. Their feet hit the back porch with a six-footed thud. Mican reached for the screen door handle and heard Mom chuckle.

"Do you three have clocks in your stomachs? Lunch is almost ready. Wash up."

They washed their hands and sat down to eat.

Mom looked at them and smiled. "So, what did the King want with you three?"

Mom listened to every word as they told her all

of the details. Her face became serious and she got quiet when they told her about dad. "I must try harder to carry on without him, but I miss him so much."

Ashton got up and went over to give her a hug. "We do too, Mom."

She wiped her eyes, sat up straight and her smile returned "So, what else did you learn?"

Shayla lifted her sleeve. "Look Momma. The King took away the mosquito-dent."

***

The next morning as he awoke, Ashton felt sad because he had not dreamed about Warrior or the King, but before he could think about it for very long, Shayla burst into his room.

Seeing Ashton awake, she leapt onto the foot of his bed. "Guess what?"

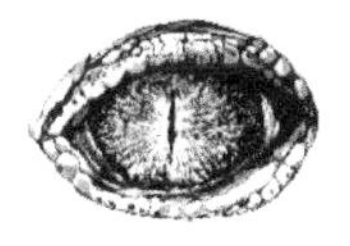

Chapter 12

Time in the Kingdom

Mican heard the noise of Shayla bouncing onto Ashton's bed and woke up.

Ashton eagerly waited, but Mican rubbed his eyes, as Shayla made her announcement.

In excitement, she bounced up and down, her voice squeaked. "Boys, he spoke to me. The King, I mean, Abba. He said we will have a word from him through the pastor today at church and we are to pay special attention."

This disclosure stirred her brothers to action. They jumped up, raced to the bathroom, and started getting ready.

Mom's voice rang out. "Breakfast."

They dashed to the table so fast they almost

overturned their chairs. Mom greeted them with wide eyes. "My goodness. You are dressed and ready to go. I'm amazed. I can hardly believe it."

***

At church, they listened attentively as the King directed Shayla in her dream. About the time they thought they'd missed it, the pastor leaned across the lecture stand that held his notes. "I have a message for you from the King."

They nearly leapt out of their seats.

The pastor lifted the King's book and extended it toward the people. "Listen closely. Every answer you are looking for is in here." He held the book with both hands, displaying it to the crowd. "Every lesson you need to learn is in here." He paused then looked down at them from behind the stand. He moved the book to point it in their direction. "Every bit of training that you need," he nodded at them, "is in here. The King sent this to you and wants you to read it. Study it. Believe it. And live it."

Whatever else he said after that blurred in their

ears. They had what they came for, a message from the King—to them. A quiet, calm came over them that their mom could not explain.

The drive to the restaurant was peaceful. They ate lunch with hardly a word spoken, except to order their food.

Mom finally asked, "What is going on with you three?"

Shayla answered. "The King spoke to me last night, he told me that today he was sending us a message, and we were to pay close attention."

Mom leaned her elbows onto the table. "Oh, he did?"

"Yes ma'am, he did."

She studied Shayla's face. "And did he? Send you a message, I mean."

"Uh-huh. We are to read his book." She added with a deep voice and great feeling, "We are to read it. Study it. Believe it. And live it." She and her mom both laughed.

***

After lunch on Sundays, it was the habit of the family to go to their rooms for some quiet time. Usually when Mom woke from her nap, she found the boys spread across their beds, fast asleep. Shayla would be in her pajamas, tucked in with her clothes folded neatly at the foot of her bed, but this afternoon, when Mom cracked the doors to their rooms, each one sat on their bed reading the King's book.

***

At dinner, Mom started a conversation. "What did the King have to say when you read his book today?" She listened closely. Each of them in turn, beginning with Mican, shared what they had read. "Tell me again about your first trip into the garden."

Ashton cringed a little at the thought of the dragon, but Mican led off telling her about the dove.

Mom heard the whole story again and confessed, "I had not realized that you were telling the absolute truth. I thought some of it was simply playing a game. So, Ashton, you really had a dream where the King called for the three of you?"

He smiled. "Yes ma'am. He's wonderful. He told us to call him Abba. That's like calling Dad, Daddy when we were younger."

She leaned in and folded her arms on the table. "I thought the King was a mean old, man waiting for us to mess up so he could punish us."

Ashton's face glowed with a warm smile. "No ma'am, he's very kind."

Shayla jumped into the conversation. "Today I read that he only corrects those he loves. And when I got Ashy into trouble, I asked the King to forgive me, and he told me that he did. He's like Dad was, he doesn't want to punish us, he wants us to learn to do better."

Mom turned her face away, but they knew tears fill her eyes. The whole family knew she had not really followed the King since Dad passed away.

Ashton signaled to Mican and Shayla to follow him and said, "Thanks for the sandwiches, Mom."

They pushed their chairs away from the table and walked into the backyard.

Ashton heard a whisper in his ear. It sounded like Abba's voice. "My, my, my, I am so blessed. What noble warriors you are becoming."

When they started to play, Shayla swung one of the plastic swords which their dad had given to the boys one Christmas. Mican picked up a stick to defend himself. Of course, Ashton grabbed the broom from the back porch and began to whip it around. The metal hanger at the top of the handle nicked Shayla on the hand and she yelped. "Ow."

Ashton froze. He dropped the broom and ran to Shayla. Blood oozed from a small scratch on her hand. "Shayla, please forgive me. I'm so sorry. I didn't mean to." Taking her by the hand he led her to the kitchen where Mom cleared the table. "Mom, help. Shayla is bleeding."

Mom wheeled around, but saw only a tad of blood. "It will be okay. It's only a scratch."

Ashton's face burned and tears filled the rims of his eyes.

His mom knelt and tried to comfort him. She

placed her hands on his shoulders. “It’s okay, Ash-bug. Shay will be fine.”

He lowered his head. “But Mom, I hurt my sister.”

Shayla pushed close to his side. “It’s okay, Ashy. I know it was an accident.”

Ashton mumbled. “But I was being my old self. I was too careless and I hurt you.”

Mican got a plastic bandage and covered Shayla’s scratch, while Mom wrapped her arms around Ashton and hugged him.

His heart pounded under the pain of what he had done.

“Ashy, I have already forgiven you, now come with me. We are going to fix this.” She took him by the wrist and led him into the backyard. With Ashton in tow, she stomped across the porch and down the wooden stairs.

“What can we do to fix it, Shay?”

“This,” declared Shayla, as she handed him the plastic sword.

Ashton’s head tilted a little and his brows

scrunched. "I don't understand. How does this fix it?"

Shayla's eyes gleamed as she picked up the broom. One eyebrow rose and she shouted. "Now run."

He whipped around and took off running with a gale of laughter trailing behind him.

As he ran, Ashton heard a whisper in his spirit. "Oh, what a girl. Part princess, part warrior, part silly child. Oh, how I cherish her. And my son Ashton, what a noble young man he is becoming."

Mican jumped into the fray, but with much more caution. They ran, and dashed, and darted, but with no one getting hurt. The prior problem had been forgiven and forgotten.

***

As future days passed, they read the King's book and discussed what they had read.

Mican had a suggestion. "Let's each keep a journal of the parts we think are meant for our training."

They agreed, but after a while they agreed to read the same passage and talk about what each learned from it. Usually they agreed on the same answer, but sometimes not.

One day when a 'sometimes not' occurred. Shayla wadded her hands into fists and placed them on her hips. "Boys, I would like to know what Abba wants us to learn from this passage."

That night, each of them prayed and asked the King to give them the answer. The next morning no one had anything to report, but Shayla had an idea. "Let's go to the castle and ask him."

The boys agreed, and with Mom's permission, they set out.

The way to the garden had become second nature to them. It took very little time to get there. After reaching the gate, they agree they would go in with faith.

The boys rolled up their shirt sleeves. Shayla took off her sweater and tied it around her waist. They glanced at each other and set to work.

They started trying to pull the vines. This time

the vines were green, but would not break, even though they pulled with all of their strength.

Shayla even grabbed a vine with both hands and placed both feet against the gate. Her feet slipped and she ended up hanging upside down. "Boys help." Her cascade of curls dangled toward the ground. Her pants legs slid toward her knees, and the sleeves of her sweater flopped toward her face like the arms of an octopus. Her body stayed in place, secured by the vine she held.

Her brothers' eyebrows shot up when they saw her.

She pressed her lips together tight, then managed to say, "This is not funny, so don't laugh."

Ashton couldn't help himself. "Well, it is really funny, Shay, but I won't laugh. I'll just chuckle instead."

They sprang to her rescue and helped her down, but still the vine she held wouldn't break. Even the boys couldn't break any vines, not a single leaf fell, so the gate remained covered.

Mican tried the slightly visible latch, but it

wouldn't move. "Man, what is up with that?"

With their heads hung low, they walked back home.

***

After dinner, they gathered in the boys' room.

Shayla tipped her head forward and had trouble looking at her brothers. "I think I know what was wrong and why the gate wouldn't open today."

"Why, Shay-belle?"

"When we came back, I went to my room, the King's book was lying open on my bed. I leaned over to close it, and I read something I had never seen before. I think it explains what happened at the gate."

"What did it say?" asked Mican.

"It said if we ask for something and our motive is wrong, we won't receive what we ask for. I had to look up what 'motive' meant. A motive is our reason for doing something. Boys, I have to confess, my reason for wanting to go to the castle was wrong. I wanted to go see Abba because I was trying to prove I was right and you were wrong and I'm sorry."

Mican lowered his head. "Me too, Shay and I'm sorry too."

They both glanced toward Ashton sprawled out on his bed. He sat up and shook his head. "Okay. Yeah, me too."

They decided they should ask Abba to forgive them. They prayed right then and there, but before they went to bed, each included it in their bedtime prayer.

Early the next morning, Shayla dashed into the boys' room and bounced on Mican's bed, then onto Ashton's. Her curls bounced higher than she did. "Get up. Get up. Get up. We have an invitation to the castle."

Moments later at breakfast, they explained to Mom what the King had shown them and told her about their new invitation.

They gobbled down breakfast, but before they dashed out, Mican turned to his mom. "By the way, I found your window-soap-vandal."

"How did you do that? Did you ask that Key-kid?

"I had already asked him. He said he saw the little kid down the street do it.

"Yeah, right. That little boy."

"I got up early this morning and looked out front. I caught him red-handed."

"Really? So, it wasn't Key-whoever?"

"No ma'am. Like he said, it was Benji, the five-year-old from down the street."

"What? Oh, my goodness. Doesn't his mother have cancer? Why would he mess up my windows, like that?"

"I asked him, he said he was trying to write, 'I love you,' to Shayla, but he doesn't

know how to write very well." Mican laughed. "Seems he is really *taken* with our girl."

Mom laughed, and everyone looked at Shayla whose face glowed pink.

"Well, I wondered why the windows were only soaped half-way up." She looked at Shayla and laughed again. "Maybe by the time he's taller, he will be able to write better, honey."

Everyone had a good laugh, except Shayla. "Okay, okay. Enough already. Let's get going. Abba is waiting."

Out the back door, they went. The screen door slammed and shouts followed. "We love you, Momma."

They raced toward the garden, but this time before they reached the gate, they received a shock—snakes covered the path, hissing and squirming.

Shayla shouted, "What do we do, bubba?"

Mican bent to pick up a strong branch. Its length almost equaled his height. He cautiously approached the nest of repulsive snakes. "Ash, grab something and help me."

"I can help with the snakes, but what do we do about the voices?"

"What voices?"

Mican strained to listen. Above the hissing, he began to pick out words.

"Gettt the kidzzz. Killll 'emmm. Stopppp the

spreadddd."

"I don't know, Ash, but help with the snakes. Maybe it's them talking."

Ashton sprang into action. "Let's get 'em, bro."

They struck the ground in front of them, as they walked side-by-side toward the squirming mass. The snakes raised their heads, hissed, and lashed out. One of them spat venom.

Mican jumped back. "Whoa, that was close. Ash, be careful." He stood his ground and shouted to her. "No, Abba invited us. There must be a way."

The dove darted into view. "Did I hear the King's name?"

They backed away for a moment and Mican said, "Yes, Shay got an invitation."

"Then allow me." The dove flew, round and round, the pile of snakes. He flew faster and faster, until the snakes spun into a wad. "Go now, children. I will hold them here."

As they ran past the knot of snakes, Ashton laughed. "Did you see that big one? Its eyes were bouncing back and forth like it was dizzy."

His sister's nose wrinkled, and the corners of her lips turned down. "I couldn't even look at those icky things. They're gross."

Within minutes, they arrived at the gate.

Mican laughed and said, "It must have heard us coming because the vines are crawling away on their own."

Ashton put his hands at his waist and blew out a long whistle. "Man that looks really strange," then he laughed, "but it's totally awesome."

When the vines had fully withdrawn from the gate, Shayla reached for the latch. The gate drifted open before her hand touched it.

They dashed inside where they found a rabbit waiting for them. "I see you have come to talk with the King."

A broad smile filled Shayla's face. "Yes, we have been invited."

"Follow me and hop to it," said the rabbit and he laughed.

Ashton returned a phony laugh. "Ha ha, very bunny."

Mican laughed. “Good one, Ash.”

Her brothers took a few steps behind the rabbit, but turned and noticed Shayla still stood at the gate with the corners of her mouth were turned down.

Mican shouted, “What’s the matter, Shay?”

“Bubba, I feel in my spirit that something is wrong. I remember Abba’s words, ‘follow my Spirit.’ Where is the dove? That’s a rabbit, not the dove.”

Mican replied, “I guess he is still twirling the snakes,” and he laughed.

A voice from behind the boys sang out. “No, here I am.” And he flew into view. “Good job, little lady. I had to sort out that ‘knot’ back there.”

Ashton laughed. “Good one.” He glanced around. “Where did the rabbit go?”

“Oh, he knew he was caught, so he hightailed it out of here.”

Shayla laughed. “Rabbit—hightailed it. That’s great, Spirit, but why is everything so funny right now?”

“Because dear one, you have the joy of the King

in you. You are filled with lightness and joy. These are rewards for work well done. Come this way, children."

Arriving at the palace, Mican asked the guard, "May we see the King?"

Shayla whispered to Ashton. "I was hoping it would be Warrior."

A handsome young man stood guard, he bowed politely, and upon rising, he swept his arm up toward the door. "Yes, you may. This way please. The King is expecting you."

Shayla nodded to her brother. "Ashy, that is what you did when we met Patrice."

He looked at her with his lips pulled tight, waiting for the laugh, but it surprised him when she managed not to giggle.

"You looked very noble, Ashy. And I'm sorry I laughed at you." His face and shoulders relaxed.

He stood up straight and smiled. "Thanks, Shay."

They approached the tall chamber doors and found them standing open. Pausing for a moment at the entrance, the King smiled and waved to them. "Come in, come in, dear ones. I have been expecting you."

Shayla started to run forward, but remembered to follow the dove who fluttered immediately ahead of her. As they arrived in front of the thrones, Shayla bent her knees, bobbed down and back up, then cheerfully greeted the King. "Hello, Abba."

The King laughed. "Hello, my little one. I see that you have learned to curtsy. Very nice."

She smiled and nodded, but her face suddenly got serious. "Abba, please forgive me for having a wrong motive when I tried to come see you yesterday."

The King leaned forward, his brows pressed close together. "I don't know what you mean, dear one."

"Don't you remember? Yesterday we tried to come see you, but the gate wouldn't let us in."

Abba leaned back on his throne, his eyes widened, and he spread his hands out to his sides. "No, I've completely forgotten."

Ashton piped in. "Do you forget a lot of things, Abba?" And he chuckled.

The King turned and stared squarely at him. "Only those things which I have been asked to forgive."

The smile disappeared from Ashton's face.

The King turned back to Shayla and smiled. "Now Shayla, as I was saying." His eyes cut to Ashton and back to her. "Yesterday you asked me to forgive you and I did. Now I have forgotten it, because when I forgive you, I remove the misdeed as far as the East is from the West. Do you understand?"

Again, she nodded and smiled. "I understand. Thank you, Abba. That is very gracious of you."

His eyes crinkled at the corners. "Thank you, dear one. Now, how may I help you today, my children?"

Ashton leaned forward. "Abba, we've been hearing voices. What are they? Or who are they?"

"The voices you hear, my boy, are followers of the dragon. The word has gone forth to stop you before you spread my word."

"What can we do about them?" asked Mican.

"If you are under my leadership, just call for my Spirit when you need help. Be cautious not to venture out into dangerous territory on your own, they cannot harm you, if you are under my protection."

Ashton tilted his head to the side. "Abba, I thought things were supposed to be easier once we became your followers."

"Ahhh, that is a common, but incorrect idea, my boy. What comes with being my follower is help in overcoming problems, not avoiding them. I will be with you always, but there will be difficulties that come. In fact, my followers often encounter more troubles, because the enemy tries to stop them from doing my will. Do you think it is worth the trouble?"

Ashton smiled broadly. "Yes, Abba. After all that you, and your Son, have done for me, I could never turn my back on you."

Abba leaned in close. "Would you turn your

back on me if it meant getting your father back?"

Ashton straightened and looked like someone had thrown cold water in his face. He turned a little pale. "Is that possible, Abba?"

"No, my son. It is appointed unto man once to die and then to stand before me,[ii] but the enemy doesn't mind lying to get my followers to turn away. My guess is, that would be the type of lie the dragon would use on you, because you have missed your father so desperately. Always be on guard, my boy."

"Thank you, Abba. I understand."

After a slight pause, Abba asked, "What else may I help you with today, children?"

They shared about how they usually agree on what a passage means, but had trouble with one where they could not agree.

"I see," said the King. "That is an easy one. Sometimes it can depend on your level of understanding and maturity."

Shayla's shoulders slumped and she sighed. "Does that mean that I didn't understand and was being childish? Is that why I didn't agree with the boys?"

"No, not at all, my child. You three were arguing over the verse, 'Where your treasure is, there your heart will be also.'"[iii] And you, my little lady, were right when you said your treasure should be in things of my Kingdom. You showed much wisdom."

She grinned and looked at her brothers.

"But," Abba looked at the boys. "Your brothers also had a good point by saying if you put things like your job above your family, then that is where your heart is. Do you not see how both can be true?"

Shayla hung her head. "It seems very clear now and our argument seems rather silly."

"Not at all, little one. You are all growing in understanding, and it pleases me that you put the things of my Kingdom as your first treasure. But your brothers were applying my word to everyday life, which also pleases me greatly. You are to live your everyday life in light of the Kingdom. Now does that settle the matter?"

They looked at each other, then back to the King. "Yes Sir, Abba. We're sorry."

Shayla smiled and added, "Thank you for another lesson."

The King returned her smile. "What else would you like to discuss while you are here today?"

Ashton lowered his head. "Sir, I mean Abba, why do I still have trouble and act like my old self? I really don't want to. I hurt Shayla by acting like my old self."

The King stared intently at him. "I saw that, Ashton, but do you want to know what stood out most to me?"

"Yes, Sir, I do."

"Your heart hurt, when you scratched Shayla. The old Ashton, as you call him, would not have been so upset. In fact, I remember another occasion when she got hurt, and I believe your words to her were, 'Suck it up, Buttercup.' Now, can you tell me the difference between those two events?"

Ashton thought hard for an answer. "I guess the

old me was not as nice to my sister as I try to be now."

"Yes, that is true. When the dragon took you, you realized in an instant you could lose her—and your brother. That showed you how much you love them and care about them. And yes, you still act like a child sometimes and children occasionally do careless things, but you are learning to defeat the old, sinful nature you call your 'old self.' What I saw when you hurt Shayla's hand was a prince, who loves his sister as if she were a princess. The prince inside you was broken-hearted when he knew he had caused his sister pain."

Ashton bowed his head. "Thank you, Abba, for seeing me that way."

"It is the only way I can see you now, my son. And I want you to remember something, what is in your mind is not always the real you. What lives in your heart and in your spirit, is the real you, and that is what I see. Don't allow the enemy to falsely accuse you in your mind. Allow your heart to grow in my word and that is what you will become. The evil one will attack your mind. Don't allow his attacks to defeat what you know in your heart."

Ashton turned to his sister. "Shay, please forgive me for when I told you, 'Suck it up, Buttercup.' I'm sorry."

With a smile and one bob of her head, she said, "I forgive you, Ashy."

Ashton turned to the King. "And Abba, I'm sorry, will you please forgive me too?"

Without delay, the King replied, "Forgiven and forgotten, my boy." The King turned to Mican. "Now my son, how can I help you?"

"Abba, when we were on our way to the garden one time, we were stopped by wolves and this time it was snakes. The dove had to come rescue us. And last time when we came into the garden, we were swarmed by gnats that bit us. When your Spirit led us back through the garden, the gnats came after us again, but the dove ate them. How can we deal with the wolves, snakes, gnats, and other creatures who try to stop us, if we run into them without your Spirit with us?"

"Well, that is a mistake, my boy. My book tells you very plainly your fight is 'not against flesh and blood,' but against spiritual forces.[iv] You should always call on my Spirit to fight for you and to guide you. Without my Spirit, you will always lose if you try to fight spiritual enemies with physical weapons. Never assume you can defeat a spiritual enemy with earthly weapons and the earthly enemies you encounter are *always* motivated by spiritual forces, so *never* try to do battle without my Spirit. Wisdom must come before warfare to be victorious."[v]

Mican nodded. "I understand, thank you, Abba."

"Abba turned his eyes toward Ashton. "And you, my boy, you must always be on your guard because you have had such a major change in your life, you are a threat to the dragon. It was he who sent the wolves to try to stop you from coming to me."

"Me, why is my change, such a threat to the dragon?"

"Because my boy, you have learned great truths.

You now have a deep understanding that even you don't fully realize yet. You, my son, will be a major force for good, as you follow me. The wolves would not hesitate to kill you, but you need not fear. That is why you must always, *always* walk in the presence of my spirit. Do you understand?"

"I understand, Abba."

Mican stared at Ashton with wide eyes, then turned his gaze to the King. "Thank you, Abba. I can see we still have a lot to learn."

For the rest of the visit, they sat at the foot of the throne and talked with the King and his Son. After a while, the King gave a nod to the guards who began opening the chamber doors. "It is time for you to return home, my dear ones."

Ashton paused with a question. "Abba, how should we ask when we want to come see you again?"

"That is simple, my boy. Any time you have something to bring before me, you can begin to thank me for the things you have and the things you have already learned. Thanksgiving is the gateway.

Then begin to tell me the things you know about me. That is praise. I'm always watching, but these things capture my attention and usher you into my court."[vi]

"Now it is time for you to go. I think there is someone waiting in the courtyard who wants to see you."

Shayla threw her fist into the air and shouted, "Warrior," but she waited to be dismissed before she rose to leave.

It took a lot of self-control to walk calmly from Abba's presence, but they managed. Upon entering the courtyard and seeing Warrior standing there, they ran toward him and surrounded him with hugs, then followed him back to the garden.

Along the way, Shayla asked a question. "Warrior, where did the dragon come from?

"Hmmm, from his cave I suppose."

Shayla tipped her head back and giggled. "No, I mean how did he get into the garden in the first place?"

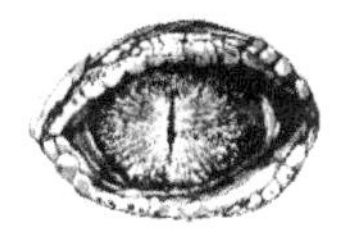

Chapter 13

The Dragon's Tale

"Many, many ages ago, a struggle came to a head in the kingdom."

Shayla stared at Warrior. "Really?"

"Yes, little one, it was started by the lead musician, who was also the worship leader for the Kingdom. He had been appointed by the King himself. The worship leader was very beautiful and very talented, but because of his beauty and talent, he fell into pride."

"It was the dragon, wasn't it?"

"Yes, it was he."

"I know what you mean," said Shayla. "I saw his original body. You know, the way he used to look."

Mican stared at her and lifted his arms to the side. "When did you see that, Shay?"

"When the dragon breathed on me and showed me the priceless stones down his back and tail, I saw him as a lovely, gleaming green being with sparkling jewels. He was very beautiful."

"Yes, dear one, that was the way he appeared before he fell into pride and rebellion. Prior to that time, all the beings of the kingdom worshipped the King and his Son. Being jealous of the King, the lead musician wanted praise and worship for himself. *He* started the war. Because of his beautiful appearance and his talent, the worship leader was able to sway one-third of the other musicians, guards, and kingdom servants to follow him in opposing the King."

Ashton rushed in front of Warrior and stared into his eyes. "Did they ever have a chance of winning against Abba?"

Warrior stopped. "No, they did not have a chance at all, but because of his pride, the worship leader thought they could win."

"What happened?" asked Mican.

"The King, Abba, had no other choice, but to throw the rebels out of the Kingdom. They were cast outside of the castle wall and driven to the far side of the garden. They were banned from ever entering the castle again, all except the worship leader, that is. Do you remember the writing on the garden gate?"

Ashton perked up. "I had forgotten about that! What does it say?"

"The message on the gate says, 'Beware the Fallen!'"

Ashton's curiosity rose. "What happened to them, the fallen, I mean?"

Warrior lowered his head. "You have met some of them in the garden. Others were given access to the people and places outside of the garden. Their primary purpose in life is to turn people away from the King."

Ashton repeated the statement. "'Their primary purpose in life *is* to turn people away from the King,'" then the words hit him with their full force.

He raised his voice. “You mean they still do that?”

“Oh yes, as you yourselves were led away by the fish, you should be able to see how they can trick people who do not follow Abba’s Spirit. Before you came to the garden, you had also met some of them in your world. The times you were tempted to disobey, or to do things you knew you shouldn’t, you were being influenced by them. Ashton, of the three of you, mainly you were targeted by them.”

“Me! Why mainly me?”

“Because you already had so much anger in your heart. You felt unloved and unwanted. Rather than accepting love, you always questioned if your brother or sister were loved more than you. You never talked to your parents about your feelings, you always hid them inside and believed the lies of the enemy. After you lost your father, the feelings only got worse. You were an easy target for the fallen ones.”

Like a light bulb turned on inside him, Ashton became aware of something, his eyes grew wide and he turned to Mican. “Bro, all the times that you were on my case to ‘do this,’ or ‘don’t do that,’ you were trying to keep me safe and I didn’t know it. I even hated you for bothering me. I see it so clearly now and I’m so sorry. Please forgive me.”

Mican’s face turned red. “Wow, Ash. I didn’t know how badly that made you feel. I’m sorry I wasn’t nicer. Will you forgive me?”

Ashton stuck his hand out. “Done, bro.” They shook and smiled at each other.

Shayla asked Warrior another question. “If there are evil fallen ones on our side of the gate, why haven’t we seen any dragons in our neighborhood?”

“There are many evil ones who roam the earth causing problems, but they don’t look like dragons. They are usually friendly and appear more pleasant, much like the little fish that you came across in the stream.”

Shayla’s forehead wrinkled. “So how can we tell the good ones from the bad ones?”

Warrior lowered his head to her level. “The first thing you must learn to do is to follow the King’s

Spirit and the words from his book. Also, you children have a good mother, so trust her to guide you, she has much wisdom because of the problems she has faced in life. These are important factors."

Warrior continued. "And as you grow in your faith, it will become clearer to you whom you can trust. Not only that, but when you ask, you will also receive wisdom from the Spirit. Just remember you must ask each time you meet a new person or a new situation. Don't ever assume that the new is the same as the old. And as you grow in your knowledge of the King and his word, it will get easier."

Ashton's face muscles tighten. "I just don't understand. Why hasn't the dragon in the garden been killed before now?"

Warrior hung his head and sighed. "The King gave him permission to live in the garden. It is he who rules the dark side of the garden and he was given the authority to send his followers into your world to trick people, to draw them away from the King. As you have already figured out, the lead musician who caused the uprising, you might even call it a war, is the dragon himself."

Shayla drew in a sharp breath. "That reminds me, I remember him singing to us in the cave. It caused me to fall asleep."

Warrior nodded. "Yes, he has a powerful gift. He can no longer live in the Kingdom, but he is still allowed to enter and come before the King to accuse people. You should have heard his argument against you three when you followed the fish."

That surprised Mican. "Abba never told us that."

"That is because you also had someone else telling him all of the good you have in your hearts."

"Really?" asked Ashton. "Who would do that for us?"

Warrior levels his eyes on Ashton. "Who do you think?"

Shayla turned to Ashton and Mican, her face lit up. "His Son. Remember when we met Abba? He said his Son had been telling him good things about us. That's who it is."

"Very good, Shayla, you are correct. There have been many times during your lives when the fallen worship leader has accused you of things."

Shayla's shoulders rose and she blurted out, "Even things we didn't do?"

"Some things you didn't do, but mostly things you did do. Each time, Abba's Son was on your side."

Ashton shook his head. "I don't understand. Why would he do that for us?"

Warrior lifted his head. "Because he loves you."

Ashton tried to understand. "You mean, he was on our side even when we were guilty of what the dragon said we did?"

"Especially, when you were guilty, Ashton. That is when you needed someone on your side the most."

Ashton lowered his head and mumbled. "That makes me love him and Abba even more, if that is possible. To be loved, then forgiven, even when I was guilty—that's amazing."

Warrior reminded him. "That is what is

available to anyone who will believe and accept the Son."

Mican threw his hands out to the side with his palms up. "How could anyone refuse that kind of love?"

The horse tried to explain. "Many people have simply never heard the truth about the King and his Son. Others are fooled by the fallen ones, then there are many people who have been so mistreated they find it hard to believe anyone can love them."

Shayla shook her head and looked at the ground. "It is sad to know that some people don't believe in, or follow Abba and his Son."

"Yes, it is dear one. If they only knew about Abba's character and his love, most people would not be able to resist. That is why people like you and your brothers are so necessary. You are kingdom warriors who will tell many people about the love of the King and his Son. But there will be some who will not listen even to you."

Ashton interrupted their conversation. "Let me ask another question about the dragon. Why didn't

Abba let the Guardian kill him?"

Warrior did his best to make it clear. "The King does not force anyone to follow him or to believe in him, that extends even to the fallen ones. The ones who pretended to want to help you: the fox, the rabbit, even the pretty fish, are some of the forms or shapes the rebels can take. They are not allowed to enter the walls around the castle, only the dragon can, but the others continue to try to fool those in your world and those who enter the garden."

Shayla bounced her hands out to the side. "You mean they can all change their shapes?"

Warrior answered. "Yes, little one, they can. Like the ugly creature whose true nature was the wicked lizard and the little fish who seemed so playful. And by the way, the frog that jumped on the rock and spoke to Mican, he was an evil one straight from the mouth of the dragon."[vii]

Mican's shoulders jumped toward his ears and he gasped. "Gosh, I didn't know that."

"You also need to know, when people think they see a dead relative, a fallen one has taken their form. Those are called familiar spirits. They pretend to be friendly, but are there to lead the person astray. The true nature of any creature can be determined by their thoughts and feeling about the King and his Son, but remember they can also lie or pretend, like the fox did. When you want to know if you can trust someone, always ask Abba's Spirit. Only he and Abba know if their hearts are pure."

Warrior continued. "Like Abba said, you must follow his Spirit. There is no way in the natural to protect yourself from being tricked. The power of the rebels is strong. That is why the King sends his Spirit to his followers. Without Abba's Spirit with you, the risk of being deceived is very high."

Shayla balled up her fists and frowned. "How can people fall for those lies?"

Warrior lowered his head. "How were you tricked by the fish?"

Shayla's mouth dropped open. "Oh my, I was tricked. How could I have forgotten?"

Warrior warned, "You must not judge those who fall for the lies. There is a war for the

Kingdom, it presents itself in crafty ways, but it is a war. It goes on constantly. You were younger and untrained when you were tricked. That is the reason you fell so easily for the lies. Shayla dear, you have learned much in a short time and are on your way to being a mighty warrior, but there is still much for you to learn." They arrived at the gate.

As the gate swung open, they gave Warrior hugs before exiting the garden. They stepped through and watched as the gate closed, separating them from their beloved friend.

Vines began to crawl up and over the gate. Ashton smiled at Mican and Shayla. "Well, that's our cue."

Side-by-side, they ran toward home. They jumped onto the back porch with their usual six-footed thud, just in time for dinner.

Mom greeted them. "Wash up, adventurers."

At dinner, they told Mom all they had learned, but Ashton had an uneasy feeling something was missing.

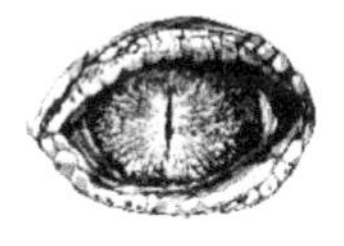

Chapter 14

Their First Assignment

The summer school bus stopped and two kids got off. When the bus pulled away, Mican stood in his front yard.

Keyon called out. “I haven't seen you in a while. I thought your mom had you tied up in the basement.”

Shayla and Ashton stepped around the corner of their house to greet their neighbors. Shayla tried to explain. “Oh no, we haven’t been in the basement, we’ve been exploring a secret garden we found.”

“Gardening, huh?” Keyon turned to Kesha and smirked.

Shayla continued. “No, we found a garden that took us to the King.” She pointed to her brother. “In the garden, Ashton was kidnapped by a dragon."

"Yeah, right, a dragon." Keyon laughed. "Did a man on a white horse rescue him?"

Shayla replied. "No, the Guardian rescued him, but he put Ashton on the King's horse, Warrior." She nodded her head with satisfaction.

"Oh brother, you guys stay by yourselves way too much. Come on Kesha, we need to get away from these weirdos."

As Keyon and Kesha walked away, Mican leaned over to his sister. "Shay, I don't think you should have started off with the part about the dragon. I don't think they believed a word you said."

Shayla plopped her arms across her body and puckered her lips. "Neither did Mom at first, remember?"

Mican noticed Ashton's quietness. "What's up, Ash?"

"Do you remember when the King told us we need to help kids who find it difficult to come to him?"

"Sure, I remember."

"Me too," added Shayla.

"I think we found our first assignment," and he pointed to the pair entering their house. "We need a lot more training before we can get them to believe us and to want to meet the King."

***

After dinner, as they discussed their day, Shayla lowered her head and stared at the floor. "Boys, I have a confession to make."

Ashton pulled his chair up next to his bed where she sat. "What is it, Shay?"

Shayla began to cry. "Oh Ashy, I know what you meant about acting like your old-self. My old-self tried to make Kesha jealous today. I need to think more about her coming to know Abba, but I wanted to make us sound special because you had escaped from the dragon."

Ashton stood next to the bed and put his arm around his sister's shoulder. "I know how you feel, Shay."

Mican asked, “Did you ask Abba to forgive you?”

She sniffed and nodded. “Yes, I did.”

“Then it’s gone,” said Mican. “Remember, ‘as far as the East is from the West.’ Now don’t let the dragon beat you up in your mind. He is trying to tell you to remember and feel bad about something that is gone and forgotten.”

“But what if she never comes to know Abba.” She burst into tears and added, “because of me.”

Ashton took her by the shoulders. “Look at me, Shayla Marie, it is not up to you whether she comes to know Abba or not. It is up to Abba, his Son, his Spirit, and Kesha. Don’t let the dragon into your head.”

“Thanks, Ashy.” She snuffled and wiped her face. “I know you are right, but now let’s ask Abba what we should do to help Kesha and Keyon come to know Him.”

They prayed long and hard before bed and prayed even more as they laid down for the night.

The next morning, they discussed a plan at

breakfast. Mom agreed they should go see the King for more training. They took the long, hot walk to the garden, but when they arrived the vines withdrew without being pulled and the gate swung inward.

"That's nice," said Ashton.

Entering the garden, they found that it felt like its usual springtime-self. They had already asked Abba to send his Spirit, so the dove fluttered toward them. "Good morning young trainees. Abba is expecting you."

Led by the Spirit, they arrived at a gorge that had a bridge across it.

Mican's shoulders pulled up slightly. "Is this part of the same ravine the dragon flew over when he kidnapped Ashton?"

"It is indeed."

Ashton shivered a bit.

Shayla tried to speed up the journey. "We've never been this way before. We are in a hurry. Can we go a faster way?"

"Slow down, little one. Abba says this is the

way I should bring you. And remember, Abba is never wrong."

"But I need to know how to talk to Kesha. She needs to come to Abba too."

The dove floated in close to her face. "We know, sweet girl. We know."

They crossed the bridge at the dove's direction. They followed along a wonderful path that led them down a hill and through a grassy plain they had never traveled before.

"Oooo, this is pretty. I'm glad we came this way. It's funny that I always like the way you take us, after we do it of course." Shayla giggled.

At the castle, a different guard met them in the courtyard. "Welcome, dear ones. I have been excited to meet you."

Surprised by his statement, Ashton asked, "You have been excited, to meet us?"

"Yes, Sir Ashton. There is much talk in the Kingdom of your growth and your abilities."

"Abilities! What abilities?"

The guard replied, "Quickly now. You mustn't

dawdle. Into the castle you go. You are expected."

Upon entering the throne room, they paused and waited to be called. Abba greeted them with a warm and loving, "Hello, warriors. Come in. I've been waiting for you."

They approached the throne with warm greetings of their own, followed by Shayla's frantic request. "Abba, we need your help. We need more training."

"I know, dear one. I heard your prayer and have forgiven you." Abba continued by explaining the best way to get young ones to turn to him. "First, you need to be a good friend and a good example. Why don't you invite them to join in games and other activities with you? When they feel safe and cared for, you can tell them about me and my book."

Shayla's shoulders popped up, the corners of her mouth turned down, and her hands sprang out in front of her knees. "But that will take so long."

"Yes, dear one. It will take some time, but it has to be. Consider how long it took each of you to come to me. And your mom and your dad before he passed away, taught you well. Some children have never had that type of training and some have even been hurt by their parents. It takes a long time to undo all of that damage."

Shayla's eyes grew wide, she leaned forward, and her voice went low. "Okay, teach us. How do we undo the damage?"

Abba smiled at her sweet, concerned face. "You can't, little one. But you can bring them to the place where, through my Spirit, I can undo the damage. That part is not your job. It is ours."

Her eyebrows knit closely together, but she answered politely. "I understand, Abba, but it is so hard to wait."

He smiled again. "I know sweet girl, but thank you for caring so much."

They remained to chat for a while. "Now it is time for you to return home. I want to thank you for taking on the task of helping to guide Keyon and Kesha to me. But a word of warning, Mican and Ashton, be careful not to be affected by Keyon's attitude. He has been greatly hurt in his life. He does not want anyone to be happy, because he is so unhappy."

Abba nodded to the guards to open the gigantic doors. "Now for my hugs, if you please." With a bright and gleaming smile, Abba spread his arms wide to receive each of them, then the dove appeared, and they followed him from the throne room.

Exiting the castle, they approached the sparkling river and turned onto a new path. Ashton's curiosity crept out. "Why do we never come or go the same way?"

The dove's eyes twinkled. "Don't you like new scenery?"

Ashton laughed. "Yeah, sure, new scenery is fine," He assumed it to be part of their training.

The dove led them to a path on the edge of some trees. He paused in front of them. "You are to go on from here alone. Stay on this path and follow no other leader, but Mican."

Mican's eyes flew open wide. He drew his neck

back tight. "Huh? What? Who me?"

"Listen with your spirit, lad. You will hear me in your heart. This will build your faith and confidence. You will be fine." The image of the dove began to fade, "If you think you need me, simply call, and I will be there," and he vanished.

"This is new," said Mican. He smiled, but his voice came out shaky. "Okay troops, listen up."

Shayla scolded him. "Mi-caaan, be serious."

"Okay, Shay. You're right. Let's stay on the path. Come on, stick close."

A bee, buzzed around Ashton's ear. He swatted it away and glared at Mican. "Why you?"

Mican replied, "What? Well, I don't know."

Shayla snapped at him. "Ashy, remember what Abba said about guarding against Keyon's bad attitude. This might be your first test."

A sting began to burn in Ashton's heart. He stared at the grass around his feet. "You might be right, Shay. I forgot how fast the tests can come." He cleared his throat, "Sorry Mican. Lead the way."

Ashton now understood. In his heart, he heard,

"Very good, my son. My warriors are learning. I'm very pleased with you."

Mican continued to lead the way through the garden. Without warning, the squadron of gnats appeared again.

Shayla dashed away and yelled. "Run!"

But Mican lifted his eyes toward the gnats and with great confidence he shouted, "Get away from us. We are under orders from the King."

The army of gnats paused in midair, lifted, then flew away.

Ashton's mouth sagged open. After a second, he said, "Wow, way to go, Mican. How did y'know to say that?"

"Thanks Ash. I heard it in my spirit, like the dove said I would. I guess we are all still learning."

They walked along in peace, but when they reached the gate Mican shared with his siblings. "What a relief. I'm surprised at how heavy the weight was on my spirit when I knew I was in charge of your safety."

Ashton apologized again and Shayla smiled.

"You boys have grown a lot. Both of you."

The gate stood open, so they rushed toward home.

They told their mom what Abba had said about being friends to Keyon and Kesha.

Mom came up with a plan. "Let's have a backyard cookout and invite them to join us."

Shayla clapped. "That's a great idea. Thanks Mom."

Mom lowered her eyes and addressed them. "I feel really bad that I thought it was Keyon who soaped my windows, but he always looks so angry, I just assumed it was him."

***

When Friday rolled around, so did the school bus. Shayla and her brothers waited to greet their neighbors.

Kesha and Keyon got off the bus.

Keyon twisted up his lips. "What's up? You guys are acting even weirder than usual."

Shayla stepped forward. "Kesha, I'm sorry I tried to make you jealous the other day. Will

you please forgive me?"

"Sure," said Kesha, but she glanced toward her brother to be sure it was okay.

Shayla stuck out her hand and presented the invitation to Kesha. It was folded and decorated with flowers.

Kesha opened it and read aloud. "My family and I would be pleased if you would join us for a cookout at our home on Saturday, at noon. The picnic will be followed by games and fun." Kesha's eyelids fluttered, then she looked toward Keyon again.

Mican reached toward him and said, "You too, Key."

Keyon opened the invitation and read. "We would like for you to come over to our house on Saturday, at noon, for hot dogs, hamburgers and games."

Keyon stared at Mican, then Ashton. "Gee guys, thanks. We would like that. We will have to ask our mom, but I'm sure it will be okay."

Mican nodded.

Keyon and Kesha turned to cross the street to their house. After unlocking the front door, Keyon looked back, smiled, and lifted his hand.

Shayla jumped up and down. Mican smiled and folded his arms, but Ashton had a strange feeling he couldn't explain.

***

Saturday rolled around and they got up early. After gobbling-down breakfast, Ashton told Mican, "I'll get the lawn bowling, water balloons, and Lawn Yahtzee games set up. Then Shay and I will set up the picnic table while you get the grill ready."

Mican said, "I can take a hint." Then he yelled, "Mom, I'm going to start getting the grill ready."

In the kitchen, she worked slicing tomatoes and onions for the burgers. "Good idea, son. Remember to clean the grill with the wire brush and stacks the charcoal in a pyramid, like dad taught you."

"I will." He retrieved the brush from the garage

and got busy scraping the surface when he heard his brother's voice.

"Bro, I'm sorry to bother you, but can we borrow your massive muscles?" Ashton grinned, made a fist and bent his arm. "Shayla is giving it her best try, but we need some help getting the picnic table moved into place. I'm afraid Shay is doing more dragging than lifting. That old table is really heavy."

"Let me clean my hands." He picked up an old towel and wiped the soot from his fingers then rubbed his palms together. The two boys made quick work of the job.

About eleven-thirty. Mom leaned out the back door. "I think you should light the coals, son."

Shayla started jumping around while Ashton set out the games.

At ten minutes till twelve, Mom took a plate of meat outside. "Mican, the fire should be ready. Will you put some hamburger patties and hot dogs on the grill?"

Shayla spun around in a circle. "Yea! I'm going

out front to watch for Kesha and

Keyon." But reaching the front porch, she saw them and their mom getting into the car. Shayla ran to the street, looked both ways, then dashed across. "Hey, did you forget the picnic?"

Their mom wiped tears from her face. "I'm sorry, I forgot to send word that they can't come. Their grandmother, my mom, is in the hospital. She is very sick and we have to get there."

Kesha turned around in the back seat and leaned her face out the window. "I'm sorry. I really wanted to come."

Keyon had his arms folded and stared straight ahead, saying nothing.

Shayla returned home with tears streaming down her face. She grabbed her mother around the waist. "They can't come."

Ashton stood on the back porch.

"What?" Mom's arms wrapped around Shayla's shoulders.

"Their grandmother is in the hospital and they have to go."

"Oh honey, I'm so sorry. I know how much you were looking forward to this."

Something struck Ashton's spirit; which one of the dragon's followers was responsible for this?

Mom went out to tell Mican what had happened and took over the grilling.

Ashton called Mican and Shayla together in his room. "Guys, I think the dragon did this to prevent us from getting closer to Keyon and Kesha."

Mican became outraged. "That dirty, rotten, evil...," then he said, "He's not going to get away with this." He began to pray.

Shayla and Ashton joined in. They got very loud.

Mican closed the prayer. "Please send your warrior angels and ministering angels to do this work. In the name of your Son, amen.

After their prayer time ended, Mom called Mican.

He went outside and asked, "Are you going to put off the picnic?"

"No, son, I promised you kids a picnic, so we

are going to have a picnic. Here, cook all of this."

The picnic went ahead as planned, but not as festive as it would have been if Keyon and Kesha had been there.

After they finished eating, Ashton wanted to know, "What are we going to do with all of these leftovers? We will have hamburgers and hot dogs for a week," and he laughed.

***

Later that afternoon, Mom gave Ashton an assignment. "Son, will you keep an eye open for when Keyon, Kesha, and their mom get home?"

***

Around five o'clock, the neighbor's car rolled down the street. Ashton stepped to the open window. "Mom, they're back."

"Thank you, Ash-bug. I've decided it's time for me to get in on this kingdom plan."

Ashton watched as she walked out of the house. A platter covered with foil lay balanced on her left arm. Atop it sat a plastic bowl filled with potato salad, and she held a bag of buns with her fingertips. In the other hand she held a plate of veggies, covered with plastic wrap. Its crowning piece—a paper plate with slices of cake.

Ashton followed her to the curb. She crossed the street as the neighbors got out of their car. "Excuse me."

Kesha's mom turned toward her.

"Hello, I'm Candice McKnight. Shayla told me your mother is in the hospital. I hope she's okay.

"She will be, thank you. She took a sudden turn for the better earlier this afternoon."

"That is wonderful news. I will be sure to share it with my family. Oh, and I thought you might be tired and might like some dinner when you got home. I hope your husband won't mind hot dogs and hamburgers?"

The lady's eyes filled with tears. "He's not here."

Candice assumed he was away on business. "I'm sorry. How long will he be gone?"

She stared down at the food. The children stood silently beside their mom. "He won't be back. He died about three months ago. He was killed in an accident at work. My Widow's Pension covers the house payment, but I had to get a job at a store near here." Her eyes puddled with tears. "When I went to see my mom today, I had to buy gas and it used up the last of our money till I get paid again tomorrow. I didn't know what we were going to have tonight for supper." She took a big breath and burst into tears. "You are a God-send."

Candice handed the food to Keyon and Kesha and gave their mom a long hug before they all went inside.

Ashton folded his arms and stared at the ground. "So that is why Keyon is so, hmmm, what?" He went into the house and called Mican and Shayla. "Mom has taken some burgers to Kesha and Keyon's mom. Let's help her with dinner. She'll be back soon."

Mican placed some burgers in the oven to warm them. Ashton got the dishes and forks. Shayla poured drinks.

A few minutes later, Mom came home with tears in her eyes. "It's a good thing we are having leftovers or I would have burnt the dinner to ashes." Then she saw what her blessings had done.

No one asked what was wrong, but finally able to talk, Mom told them the whole story. "Their grandmother is much better. Keyon and Kesha's mom's name is KeLesha Stone and their dad past away about 3 months ago."

Mican looked at his siblings, then back to her. "We're happy to hear that their grandmother is better."

Ashton wondered if her improvement followed their prayer time, but he kept it to himself.

Mican stared at the table. "Mom, I can't believe that we didn't know about their dad. When we lost our dad, people came by and brought tons of food. I've never seen anyone over at their house."

"I know, son. It broke my heart too."

That night, in Shayla's room, they sat on the bed and talked.

Ashton spun the fuzzy, pink pillow in his hands. "Now I understand why Keyon can be so…."

They decided, *hard to get along with*, would be a good way to put it.

Mican added, "Now I know how Keyon has been so hurt. And guys, did you notice their last name?"

"Sure," said Shayla. "It's Stone. Kesha and Keyon." She smiled. "You call him Key." She gasped. "Do you think they are the Key Stone kids those creatures were talking about."

"Bingo!"

"You're brilliant, bro," said Ashton. "If we get stopped, those voices, think that the Stones will never come to know Abba. Man, we need to pray."

They each took a turn praying for Keyon, Kesha, their mom, and their grandmother.

***

For many months, Mican, Ashton, and Shayla read the King's book faithfully and prayed many times during their days. Sometimes they shared what they learned, but each kept their own journal. They made special efforts to include Keyon and Kesha in their plans whenever they could. And occasionally KeLesha found a few much-needed bags of groceries on their porch.

Over those months, the cold weather and rain only allowed Mican, Ashton, and Shayla to make a few visits to the castle.

Mican decided to talk to his brother and sister about the situation. “Guys, as our visits to the castle have become less frequent, I’m not sure I’m growing as much spiritually, as I once did.”

They met together and prayed about it.

That night, Mican heard from the King. As the sun rose, so did he. He received a dream of a special invitation for all three of them to visit Abba. He excitedly wondered what the King had in store for them this time?

Chapter 15

Three Thrones

Mican went into the kitchen to prepare breakfast. Mom had the coffee pot set on a timer, so as it brewed, she awoke. Entering the kitchen, Mom found Mican had set the table and poured juice for the family. Her eyes opened wide. "What's this?"

"Good morning to you too," said Mican with a chuckle.

With a sheepish grin and a sparkle in her voice, Mom said, "Good morning, son. Thank you for fixing breakfast. You have grown so much. Is there a special occasion this morning?"

"Yes, ma'am. I had a dream. The King asked us to come for a visit. It has been one year since we were first led to the gate. Would you like to come with us? I'm sure it will be okay."

Mom walked over to Mican and gave her tall, lean, fourteen-year-old son a big hug. "Thank you, young man, but I have things here I need to take care of. You three go ahead and enjoy your visit." She pushed away and brushed a tear from her cheek.

***

After breakfast, Mican, Ashton, and Shayla headed toward the garden.

Ashton bounced along the path. "I can hardly believe it has been a year already." He glanced at his siblings and could see changes in them. Shayla had grown so much. Mican had gotten taller, and had a whisker or two, that he proudly shaved—once a week. "Guys, I can see a lot of difference in you two, but I can't tell as much difference in myself." He wondered if they could, but it was too late to ask, they arrived at the gate.

Mican stretched out his hand, but the green, twisted branches crawled away, and the gate swung open. They entered the now familiar area and scanned it. The weather felt spring-like here, though winter had recently closed out on their side of the gate.

"No one has come to meet us." Mican scratched his chin. "Hmmm, that's odd. No Warrior, no dove, not even a false bunny."

With his eyes shut, Ashton stuck his hands out to his brother and sister. "We need to pray."

When they opened their eyes, the dove hovered next to Ashton.

Shayla placed her hands on her hips and looked at him. "You're late."

"That is quite impossible, my little lady. I assure you at the very instant Ashton asked the King for guidance, he sent me."

"Oh!" Shayla hung her head. "I'm sorry."

"You see, young one, you can never assume that I will be waiting. The truth is Abba is waiting for you to ask for me. I only come when you ask, or the King sends me on his business."

"I see the truth of that," said Shayla. "Thank

you for the lesson, Spirit."

"Come now, the King is waiting." The dove turned and started down an unfamiliar path.

Ashton laughed. "I see that you have found another way we have never been before."

The dove joyfully replied. "You will experience many paths as you travel through life, but there is only one way to the throne room of the King and each of you has found it."

With a hint of fear in her voice, Shayla asked, "Why are we going *this* way?"

"Fear not, sweet girl. You are quite safe in the King's care. Simply be obedient. Do exactly as I say."

They obeyed completely and on the other side of the ridge, they could see the castle in the distance.

"Awesome!" exclaimed Ashton.

"This is amazing," said Mican.

Shayla replied, "It's so beautiful." Then she added, "I'm glad we came this way, Spirit."

"Yes, my little lady, you will see many wonders

as you follow Abba through your lives. Now quickly, down this path."

They arrived safely at the castle gate, which opened as they stepped toward it. Once inside, the Spirit directed them. "You know the way."

The grand castle door opened and they stepped inside. When they reached the inner doors, they already stood open.

Mican whispered, "I see we are expected."

The King greeted them with a sunny smile. "Please, come in. I've been waiting for you."

They rushed forward and greeted Abba with love and excitement.

"Thank you for calling us," said Mican.

"It is my pleasure, lad. I always enjoy our time together. And I have a new topic for your lesson today. Mican, do you remember, in my book, when my Son said that he is the 'door'?"[viii]

Mican nodded vigorously. "Yes, Abba, I do."

The King continued, "Have you ever wondered what that means?"

"No, Sir, it means that he is the way for us, the

sheep," and Mican grinned, "to enter in or come to you."

"Yes, that is very good. But earlier you were reading the passage in my book that tells you to lift up your heads 'oh, you gates,' then it says to lift up your heads 'you everlasting doors' and the 'King of Glory shall come in.'[ix]

"Do you know who the King of Glory is?"

Mican smiled. "Sure, you are, Abba."

"That is correct, but then you questioned who the 'gates' and 'doors' are."

"Yes, Sir."

"Since you know that the main door is my Son and that I am the King of Glory, can you figure out who the 'gates' and 'doors' are in that song?"

Mican thought for a minute. He pulled his eyebrows close together. "Is it us? I mean, your followers? Are we the gates and doors that are supposed to lift up our heads, so you can come in?"

"Yes, indeed, young man. Very good. That part of my word refers to my followers, lifting up their heads, or looking to me, and asking me to come in.

You, my warriors, are the gates and doors. You may lift up your heads and ask me to come in by using praise, worship, and prayer. You can do much to bring my presence into your world. Seek me continually and ask me into every situation in which you find yourselves."

Mican smiled and nodded, "I understand Abba and I will."

Abba smiled and glanced toward Ashton and Shayla. "That goes for you two as well. It is available to all of my warriors."

They nodded. "Yes, Abba. We understand."

"Another lesson for each of you is to remember to watch your words. Life and death are in the power of your tongue."[x]

Again, Ashton couldn't resist. "How do we watch what we can't see, Abba?"

Abba turned to him, but instead of frowning, he smiled. "I think you might be able to figure out what I meant, Ashton."

He glanced down at the marble floor and his cheeks flashed hot. "Yes, Sir, you mean for us to be aware of what we say."

"Yes, my dear warrior, words have power."

"When you say you can't do something, you probably will not be able to do it. You need to speak strength to yourselves. I want you to do well. I want you to succeed." Abba smiled and stared at his followers. "Please know that I always want my blessings to rest on you." His big bushy eyebrows came close together and a serious expression covered his face. He leaned forward. "And remember your words—*will—always—invite—someone—in*."

Ashton's eyes popped open wide. "What?"

"You are a gateway, my son, watch your words and be careful who you invite to cross through your gate. Also, be careful what posters you put on your walls and what you watch on television or at the movies. You are mine and the enemy will search for ways to take your eyes off of me and my plans for you."

Ashton glanced from Mican to Shayla and they nodded. "We will Abba, I'm sorry I made a joke."

The King grinned and spoke directly to him. "No need to apologize my son. I made you. I made you with a sense of humor. Only be sure you use it at the proper time and in the proper way. I love your spirit and your humor, my boy. And your talent as an artist is wonderful."

Ashton grinned. "Really? Thank you, Abba. I love you so much."

"You are quite welcome, my warrior. Now I have another new lesson for you three today. And I have prepared some special seats for you."

Without even the slightest sound, three small golden thrones appeared behind them. Abba gestured for them to turn around. "Please be seated."

Completely amazed, they slowly took their seats facing the King. Abba watched them with a warm smile, then he sat up straight on his throne and gently gave a command. "Mican, please stand."

As Mican rose, a mist formed behind Abba's throne. It became like a screen in a movie theater. Mican stood speechless. Before his eyes, a picture of himself as a baby appeared. Next, he watched the pictures, as he grew into a toddler and then as a young child.

The pictures advanced all the way to his current age, but didn't stop there. His image continued to change and mature until he saw himself as a man, dressed in a suit, and talking to some people in what appeared to be a large meeting room in an office building.

"This is how I see you even now, my son. I know you as you were, as you are, and as you shall be. The man you are becoming pleases me very much."

As the mist faded, Mican said, "Thank you Abba, but why did you show me this?"

"I want you to know that you have a bright future, just as your Grammy told you. Stay close to me, as I know you will. It will ensure your future will be a bright one."

Mican smiled. "Thank you, Abba."

"My pleasure, son. You may be seated."

He took his seat once again, as Abba called his

brother's name. "Ashton, will you stand before me."

Ashton promptly stood. Again, behind the throne a mist rose. The face of a baby appeared, next the image changed to a small child, then all the way to his present thirteen-year-old self.

Again, the pictures continued to age and mature. Like Mican, Ashton watched himself as he became an adult. He couldn't help but comment. "In this picture, it looks like I am surrounded by family, friends, and children. The scene looks like it is at Christmas and I'm in a lovely home."

Abba smiled. "That is true, my boy."

A calm feeling came over him. "Wow, I feel amazing, even now, just seeing this."

"Ashton, my warrior, you have grown so much. I am very pleased. You, more than your brother and sister, have worried about being loved and accepted. Know this, my son. You are deeply loved. You have a bright and wonderful future ahead of you, if you stay close to me, as I know you will."

Tears filled the rims of his eyes. "Thank you, Abba. You are my best friend."

As he took his seat, Shayla popped up before the King called her name.

Abba tossed his head back and laughed. “Excited, are we?”

“Yes Sir, I want to see.” The mist began to form behind the throne. Shayla’s pictures moved across the screen. First as a baby, then the images changed, and changed again. They zipped right past her eleven-year-old-self until she saw herself as a mature, lovely, young woman. In the picture, she appeared to be in her early thirties. Behind her stood a man holding a small child, but they were blurred by the mist.

Shayla squinted and complained. “Abba, I can’t see what they look like.”

“I know, little one, but that is all I want you to know at this time. If you knew more, you would constantly be trying to make it come to pass. But I want you to know you have a nice future and a family to come. Keep your eyes on me. Wait for *me* to work it out. It will be awhile, but wait, Shayla. Remember, don’t run ahead of my Spirit.”

Shayla smiled. "Thank you, Abba," and returned to her seat.

The King leaned back on his throne. "What a marvelous time I have had with you three today. You have each grown so much and I am very pleased with you. I believe it is only right that from this day forward, I will no longer refer to you as children. I will call you my Mighty Ones, but never forget, the stronger you grow in my word, the more the enemy will come after you. He will never stop. And I want to remind you, do not fight him in your own strength. You must always call on me, my Son, and my Spirit to fight for you."

Ashton glanced at his siblings, then he looked back at the King. "We will remember, Abba."

"Now rise, Mighty Ones, it is time for you to return home."

They stood and Shayla curtsied. "Abba, may I give you a hug before we leave?"

"Why, certainly, Mighty One. Yes, indeed, all of my Mighty Ones may hug me. You will never be too old for that."

Before they left his presence, they each gave the King a big hug.

They followed the Spirit out and around the other side of the lake and through the hills this time, but they had to cross the same gorge as before.

Once they entered an open space in the garden, the dove began to spin around in the air. Astonished, they stopped and stared at him.

Mican asked, "Ash, what do you think the dove is doing?"

The dove streaked toward Ashton and zoomed around his head in a circle. All of a sudden, Ashton began to spin around and dance. He had a smile on his face that reached from ear-to-ear.

Mican turned to his sister. "Shay, do you think he hears music? I can't hear anything. Do you?"

"I don't hear anything, except the breeze, bubba."

Ashton threw his hands out to the side and whirled around. They stepped back a few feet to give him room, but suddenly, he stopped stone-still.

Chapter 16

The Awakening

The dragon stomped his way out of the forest. Shayla gasped and stepped closer to Mican, but the dragon stared only at Ashton. "I see that you are trespassing again in my garden."

Shayla grabbed Mican's arm and shouted. "We are not trespassing. We were invited here."

Out of the corner of his eye, Mican noticed an ugly reptile slinking toward them. "Shay, get behind me."

"I can't. The weasel is sneaking up back there."

Mican glanced around. He pushed her to his side, but before she found her footing, she stumbled and fell.

An army of ants, scurried toward her from the

front. She screamed and tried to stand, but looking up she yelled. “Mosquitoes!” The scourge of mosquitoes swarmed above her in a circle. The gigantic ants surrounded her on the ground. A boa-constrictor slithered toward her.

More creatures joined in, while other intruders surrounded Mican. Huge rats, snakes, and badgers, along with toads, lizards, and bats gathered.

Ashton seemed not to notice their plight. He took a step toward the dragon. “Don’t argue with him, Shay. We have no need to explain anything.”

The dragon thrust his neck forward and smoke billowed from his nostrils. “So, you don’t think you need to explain. Well, I think you need to do a lot more than that.”

When Ashton took another step closer, the dragon drew his head back and opened his mouth to deliver a fiery blast.

Mican and Shayla, stunned, trapped and helpless, watched Ashton as he strode toward the serpent. “You are right, dragon. I do need to do more than explain. I need to tell you something.”

"I need to tell you something too, boy. My followers have your brother and sister surrounded."

Ashton smiled, but didn't even glance in their direction. "Make no mistake about it, your disgusting followers will not harm my brother or my sister. We are under the protection of the King. Now you listen to me."

The dragon glared at him like he was a mid-day snack, then addressed him with a snarl. "What do you need to tell me, silly child?"

Ashton stood tall and shouted into the face of the dragon. "You are on the King's land. You have no authority here. We are under the direction of the King and his Son. You *will* leave us alone." He yelled even louder. "In the name of the King, you have to go. Now!"

The dragon's jaw went slack and his eyes widened. With Ashton's confidence and the King's Spirit being with him, the dragon had no choice. "This is not over, little boy. You *will* taste my anger. You will have to watch your back for the rest of your life."

Ashton lifted his arm and with a downward swat, he said, "Yeah, yeah, we know. The King told us."

The dragon nodded toward his minions, giving a signal, but he turned to slither away.

Shayla yelled, "Ashy, help. We are trapped."

Ashton turned and faced her for the first time. She screamed, "Ashy, help me!"

As smooth as silk, he replied, "You don't need me, Mighty One. Rise up and take authority, in the name of your King."

A peaceful look came over her face; her shoulders eased down, she pointed at the swarm of mosquitoes and lifted her voice. "In the name of the King and his Son, get—away—from me."

The swarm lifted and made a beeline into the woods.

She stood, turned her eyes to the ground and shouted. "Ants, you have no place here. This is the Kings land. Leave. Now!"

Ashton shouted, "Good work, Mighty One. I've never seen ants run so fast," and he burst out laughing.

The boa constrictor crawled across the toe of her shoes. She lifted her foot and tossed him to the side. “Be gone vile creature. Go back to the dark side of the garden, in the name of the King.”

The snake raised its head, made eye contact with her, but turned and slithered away.

Ashton smiled at her with pride. “Good job, Mighty One.” He turned to Mican, still surrounded by drooling, growling creatures. He folded his arms. “Well, bro?”

A peace came over Mican. He lifted his hand and pointed at each creature. “In the name of the King and his Son, whom I believe in with all of my heart, you must go. Be gone.”

They snarled and growled, but had no choice except to back away.

The dove darted toward Ashton and patted him on the back with a feathered wing, “Well done, Mighty One. Very well done indeed. And well done, Mighty One Shayla and Mighty One Mican. The King is very pleased.”

"Thank you, Spirit." Ashton turned to face the path again.

Mican raced toward him and pulled him around by the shoulder. "Whoa, Dude, what came over you? What was all that spinning about before the dragon showed up? And how did you know what to do?"

Ashton stopped and glanced from his brother to his sister. With their eyes firmly fixed on him, he lifted his hands and asked, "Didn't you hear the singing? It was like a choir of angels, but not girls, it was men—warriors—lifting their voices in praise to the King. When the dove spun around my head, I just had to dance. Y'know, like King David did in Abba's book."[xi]

"What?" asked Mican.

"Don't you get it? I needed to join in. It was pure praise to Abba, I guess you would say. Then Abba spoke to me in my heart and said, 'Rise up like a warrior.' So, I did."

Mican and Shayla's mouths never closed, so he continued. "Y'know, before I met the King, I thought I was a coucamou, but now I know that all I am is because of him. All of the praise goes to Abba. He made me. I'm nothing without him."

Shayla twisted up her lips, her eyebrows went all wavy. "You thought you were a what?"

Ashton tipped his chin up and howled with laughter. "A coucamou. Because I thought I was as fast as a cougar, sneaky as a cat, and quiet as a mouse. That would make me a coucamou. Get it?" He laughed again and returned to the path.

Speechless, Mican and Shayla just stared at each other, then fell in line walking behind their brother. As they walked through the garden, Ashton shouted and leapt along the path.

Suddenly, Ashton stopped.

Then they heard Abba's voice. It started off like a low rumble, then it burst into a clap of thunder and proclaimed, "The Sleeper Awakens!"

Ashton paused, grinned, then sprinted toward the gate with a whoop. When they reached the gate, it opened before them.

Mican and Ashton walked through—sort of.

Actually, Ashton sprang through.

They stood outside, while Shayla spoke to the Spirit.

The dove fluttered close to her ear and gently gave her a peck on the cheek. With the tone of a parent he said, “Mighty One, I am so proud of you. I will always be with you. Rest assured, I am only a whisper away.”

“Thank you, Spirit. I wish I could give you a hug.”

He replied, “Allow me.” He placed one wing on the back of her head, the other wing covered her whole face. It appeared really funny, like she wore a feathered cap that slid down over her face.

Ashton had to put his hand over his mouth, so he wouldn’t laugh. He and Mican waited respectfully outside the gate.

When the hug ended, Shayla smiled and giggled. “That tickled. Thank you, Spirit.”

She dashed through the gate to join her waiting brothers.

The gate swung toward them, when the latch

clicked, vines began to crawl up and over the familiar wooden structure.

"I just love watching that," said Ashton.

As they turned to head toward home, Shayla stepped between Mican and Ashton and hooked her arms in theirs. "Come on, Mighty Ones. Let's get home. Mom will want to hear all about our day."

They took a few steps, but Mican stopped. He tilted his ear up, as if listening to something.

Ashton and Shayla stood watching.

Mican's eyes closed and a pale outline of the dove hovered above his ear.

Ashton whispered to Shayla. "I wonder what's up?"

Shayla smiled at him and returned a whisper.

"Guess we will have to wait to see, huh?"

Not Nearly the End

Author Bio

June Whatley has taught first through third grades in a Christian school; she has also taught Middle Graders in two different Christian schools; and has taught Study Skills in the Remedial Developmental Department of the third largest college in Tennessee.

Mrs. Whatley holds a combination Master of Arts degree in Counseling and Education from Regent University in Virginia Beach, Virginia.

June is a wife, mother and grandmother of four of the greatest Grands in history.

Endnotes

[i] Christy King Griffith.

[ii] Hebrews 9:27.

[iii] Matthew 6:21.

[iv] Ephesians 6:12.

[v] Pastor Ed Griffith.

[vi] Psalm 100:4.

[vii] Revelation 16:13.

[viii] John 10:7.

[ix] Psalm 24:7-9.

[x] Proverbs 18:21.

[xi] 2 Samuel 6:14.